GW00367786

To Marzai

With affn

NEW CREATION

A Novel

John Poynton

John Poynton's novel *New Creation* is written in the great tradition of the classical journey of the hero. Tracking the deepening inner experiences of a young game ranger's passage through the surviving landscapes of the African wilderness, the narrative challenges the modern veneration of science and technology at the expense of the values of spiritual generosity and the conservation of the natural order. John Poynton is highly qualified as a guide and mentor on this particular journey. Professor Emeritus at the University of Natal, research associate of the Natural History Museum and scientific fellow of the Zoological Society of London, Secretary and former President of the Society for Psychical Research in London, he has made significant contributions to both biological and psychical research. He writes with the authenticity of personal experience. *New Creation* is a compelling read in this era of accelerating ecological crisis and global climate change.

Graham S. Saayman
Professor of Psychology, University of Cape Town (1974 – 1989)

New Creation

Published by:
The Power of Words, an imprint of Kima Global Publishers

Kima Global House,
50, Clovelly Road,
Clovelly
7975
South Africa

© John Poynton 2012

ISBN: 978-1-920535-19-3

First edition April 2012

email: info@kimaglobal.co.za
web site: www.kimaglobalbooks.com
Cover design by Nadine May

With the exception of small passages quoted for review purposes, this edition may not be reproduced, translated, adapted, copied, stored in a retrieval system or transmitted in any form or through any means including mechanical, electronic, photocopying or otherwise without the permission of the publishers.

New Creation

A Novel

by

John Poynton

To the memory of Michael Whiteman 1906 – 2007
Mystic, musician, mathematician, philosopher
Citizen of Cape Town, inhabitant of many worlds

PART ONE

Chapter One

It was still alive, spotty brown fur rumpled on bone, the starved remains of a lion cub. If it had any strength it would have lashed tormentedly at flies scrabbling over its eyes, nostrils, its mouth, but sprawled there under a thorn-bush in blazing African heat, it hardly breathed.

The game reserve's head guard, thickset Makanya, peered under the bush at the cub.

'Auu …' For a strong-voiced talker like Makanya the groan told of things too heavy for words to carry. He turned his bulldog head to look away, to look anywhere except at the cub we had been searching for. Yet Nsundu unslung the rifle from his shoulder, Nsundu, slender and moving easefully like a zebra stallion, the game ranger who had the job of breaking me in as a ranger. He and Makanya were taking me on my first foot patrol along the northern boundary of the game reserve.

And here in the heat we had found this cub abandoned by its mother, dying under a thick buzz of flies.

As Nsundu raised his rifle, 'Is that all we can do?'I asked. 'Just stand there and shoot it?'

Rifle lowered, Nsundu turned to me perhaps wondering if the son of a mission teacher could ever make a good game ranger. Carry it to camp? the blankness of his look was asking. It would be dead by the time we reached there. Give it more disturbance, fear than it need have?

And for Nsundu also not to speak meant, talking leaves only dryness in your mouth.

'But …' This abandoned cub. Protect the game – isn't that why I had joined the Game Department? 'But don't we have to do *something*?'

Nsundu sounded impassive. 'Do what thing?'

We were speaking Zulu, a language tuned to the vast spaces of Africa, yet what use is any language when you have no ideas for it to handle?

The cub had been found only by chance. Foot patrol had been the drill on this my fifth day as a ranger: scout for poachers, look for snares, check boundary fences, protect the game. Protect … the word was to grow an uncertain meaning under the scorching midday sun as the three of us had been trudging through dry bush-clumps on patrol along the boundary fence.

'We must go carefully here,' Makanya had said as we came near this place. His way of speaking Zulu was gruff, tough like the way he looked. 'Here a lioness gave birth to cubs – right against the fence. Does she have worms in her head?'

'That lioness!' Nsundu was laughing at that stage. 'Me, if I were a lion, I'd give no cattle in bride payment for a wife like that. I tell you, this is the same one that abandoned her last litter.'

'I wonder if we'll be able to see the cubs,' I said expectantly.

Makanya was also laughing. 'You'll see nothing but the lioness's jaws if you don't walk carefully. And that will be the end of your new life as a ranger!'

So we carried on warily. In this bush you do not see things even a metre away – perhaps not even the tawny body of a lioness among waving grass and twiggy thickets.

We searched the ground for spoor. All kinds of animals had left fresh tracks here, but no sign of lion. A quick dart ahead of us and something vanished. A bushbuck, perhaps? One could not see. 'Bad place to meet a rhino,' Makanya rumbled. 'No trees big enough to climb to get out of its way.'

Nsundu laughed again. 'You watch – we'd even climb the air like winged baboons if a rhino came at us.' Nsundu had a sense of the ridiculous; he pawed the air as if running up it.

A raiding party of meerkats bundled away from us, tails up like flagpoles. Now bigger animals showing above grass in a clearing. Three hyaenas.

'Careful.' Nsundu put out a hand to stop me. 'See, there is something here the hyaenas themselves have killed. It's not a lion kill; the vultures are not here yet.'

We drew closer – then almost automatically took a few paces back to the cover of a thicket.

'Hau!' Makanya said quietly. 'I too, if I were a lion, I would not give any bride payment for that lioness.'

The hyaenas were eating what must have been one of her cubs.

'There were two cubs,' Nsundu said.

'Then what about the other?' I asked.

Nsundu merely grunted. Yes, where would you start to look?

'Isn't there just a chance?' I said. 'It could be in one of those thickets. Perhaps …' Perhaps the cub had been eaten already. Perhaps anything. I turned round unsurely to Nsundu.

He waved me to silence, cupped his hands to his ears to listen. Then, 'There,' he whispered, now half crouching. 'That thicket, there.'

I'd heard nothing, but we followed him – for some reason we were all crouching – to a thicket five metres from the hyaenas. There we started searching.

It must have been the buzz of flies that Nsundu heard, not any sound from the cub itself. It seemed beyond that. I looked towards the hyaenas. 'Let nature take its course,' you'd hear people say over a beer back at camp, 'let hyaenas eat the cub alive.' But beer-talk blinds you to tragedy. And 'Protect the game,' another thing you heard; but protect the game from what? You can't protect this cub even against its own mother, let alone against everything else in the reserve that was out for a scrap of food or a bit of moisture. I turned away as Makanya had done to gaze around me at the bush quivering in the heat. If you can't protect the game against itself, then why bother to protect it against people who come to poach it?

Nsundu aimed his rifle and again I looked away, trying also to look away from a question that hovered like a vulture over the cub: why bother to protect what is senseless, going all wrong? And now, standing here and staring at the wound in the middle of the cub's head, here were questions suddenly woken to, questions seen from the inside, questions that were not among the stuff packed in the mission Land Rover the day I headed towards the reserve. Five days ago – there seemed no place for questions then as my father and I sped over the dusty road from the mission station to the reserve, some ninety kilometres away. Twenty-one years old and the life of a game ranger ahead, I was in such a hurry to get here that my father beside me in the passenger seat kept saying 'Don't drive so *fast*, Robert. You'll wreck this thing by the time we reach the reserve, and then how do I get back to the mission?'

Five hot days ago. As we sped that day to the reserve we slowed down only on the ridge in this gigantic plain from where you see the reserve gates, and the clustered huts of a guard camp a little way beyond. Here we paused, took time to gaze in silence across the plain. As I stopped the Land Rover the whole scene shimmered in the heated midday air, brooding, remote at this distance even if exploding on every sense of someone making his way through it. Some eighty years ago this wild magic had stirred enough people to fight for its survival; it was unused land then, with a potential for bringing tourist wealth to the district. And now, as we paused a moment on the ridge, the outcome lay before us, a stretch of dark and light green saved from the earth-brown cancer that crept through land around it.

Far over towards the middle of the reserve on slightly raised ground you can see the rest camp. Beyond it the greenness spreads away without a break of water, but just this side of the camp flows a river. It is bordered by a floodplain that collects huge water-filled pans now glinting through the haze, and here and there the river shows through its dark-green cloak of giant sycamore fig-trees. The pans, with their surrounding groves of greeny-yellow fever-trees, are a wonderland of birds and the watering place for thriving herds of game.

As I started the engine to drive down to the gates my thoughts had already jumped ahead to explore the world soon to be my home: the game, the poachers, the tourists, the life at the rest camp, the game guards and rangers – I knew them because we were frequent visitors from my father's mission. Yes, people like Makanya, Nsundu, and perhaps more than anyone, the chief ranger, John Duma. Was my new job really taking me to the reserve or to the chief? In a way there was no clear difference; so much in the reserve seemed to turn round him. So much, even to a quick turn-over of ranging staff. I was not the only new replacement. A month ago there had been another switch and, 'Wish me luck,' I said to my father as we drew up at the reserve gates. 'I hope I won't come spinning out of here in a couple of weeks' time with the chief ranger after me.'

My father passed a hand thoughtfully through his greying, close-cut hair. He was about to say something, but sank back in silence. There were still ruffled feelings about what I should be doing in life. Should I be a worker in the crop of souls around my father's mission, or should I take up the real mission in my life – as I saw it – to salvage bits of wildlife scattered behind the swelling tide of man? At the mission I had the job of estate manager; enough scope there for conservation, they said. I tried to start a nature reserve in one corner, yet at the mission they also said that man's needs must rate higher than those of nature. If man had been created in God's image, then how can you give space to a lower creation when the supply of land runs out? And distending families round the mission were swamping even farmland.

So I had chosen the game reserve, where the supply of land had not yet run out. The day we drove to the reserve, the question of where I should be working seemed at last to be settling with the dust thrown up behind us. The act of driving itself was final; I was to become a ranger, and the mission could do without me. Now the reserve gates were being opened by a game guard, giving a beaming salute and the Zulu 'I see you! The Fawn-who-sits-by-himself,' the name given by game guards when I came here as a boy. Typical of African names it showed frank observation; they knew me as one who keeps to himself, absorbing the bush in silence.

My father gave the guard a sideways look. 'Me, I say his name is: The Fawn-who-turns-his-father's-car-into-smoke.'

'Hau!' The guard laughed and pointed to a 40 km/h speed restriction sign. 'The chief will turn *him* into smoke if he catches him speeding in the reserve.'

I looked up at the burning sun. 'If the chief catches me I'll just say, "I don't want to fry on this road".'

Another laugh as the guard closed the gates behind us. 'At least you won't run down any game. Beasts –' he pointed to the sun – 'beasts also don't like frying on the road. Everything will be lying up in the bush; you'll be lucky if you see even a warthog on your way to camp.'

And a warthog trotting with tail erect across the road was about all we did see before the camp came into sight.

Thirty-five huts are bunched there to house tourists, substantial little buildings despite the name 'hut', with whitewashed walls and peaked, thatched roofs. Beside them are staff and administration buildings. I drew up at the hut marked Office, and Sibanda appeared in the doorway, Sibanda the One-very-clever-like-a-lizard, who had left a store-keeping job eight years ago to take up the post of camp superintendent. Now he stood gravely surveying the Land Rover, his trim forty-year-old frame stooped in his favourite act of weathering a mock crisis.

'Morning, Mr McBraid.' He always spoke to my father in English. 'Where does your car keep its wings?'

'What do you mean?' my father asked in his soft Scottish accent after returning the greeting.

Sibanda came to his side of the cab.

'The bridge – miracle it carried you. Last night –' arms were flung down to show a collapse – 'last night it was almost washed away. Big big storm. Hello Robbie!' He looked through the cab window towards me. 'You've come just in time for heavy work.'

'The bridge seemed all right to me,' I said getting out of the Land Rover.

'Eah!' Sibanda opened the door for my father. 'Big flood, and now – everywhere there's mess. You didn't see the chief in trouble? At the pan near the camp gates? A rhino stuck there in mud.'

As my father climbed out of the Land Rover he muttered, 'I regret to say that my young Robert was driving so fast, we couldn't see anything.'

Sibanda shook his head. 'Tsk tsk. Then let's hope the chief didn't see your Robert.'

He laughed and pointed to a hut just beyond the chief ranger's house. 'Robbie, that's where you stay. You can take your things there. Soon the chief will be back.'

My father looked uneasily at his watch. 'Soon? Has Duma said when that will be?'

He used John Duma's family name, which seems right for a word that in Zulu means thunder.

'He said,wait in his house for him. He won't be long.'

Sibanda led my father to Duma's house while I drove round to my hut.

So, this is where I was to live – the nearest building to the chief's house. Only a stone's throw away, and I knew he would make use of that: 'Hey, Rob!,' a crash against the door near midnight, and we would be off on one of those wild moonlight patrols that send the magic of Africa pouring through your veins.

A moment to press my hand in greeting against a towering fig-tree outside my door – the tree would probably shake with fruit-bats that night – and I hurried over to Duma's house.

My father had just steadied himself after a welcome from Duma's two hefty ridgeback dogs, and was settling into a cane chair in the sitting-room.

'Evidently the chief's not married yet,' he remarked to Sibanda as he looked round the room, a jumble of cane and upholstered chairs, randomly scattered coffee tables and a small fridge for drinks. 'And – he's over thirty, now, isn't he? – one wonders about the chances of his ever getting married.'

Sibanda was standing just inside the front door. He opened out his hands to show there was a problem. 'His mother a White; father Zulu, does that make a match easy?'

My father glanced down at the floor half muttering, 'One would like to say nowadays that's no difficulty at all, but … tribal thinking.'

He looked back at Sibanda saying, 'Your chief personifies many trends of our times, does he not?'

Sibanda wore a fateful look. 'There's a price to pay for that. Anyway –' he was brightening again – 'you'd need a lion-tamer to match him. Well Robbie,' he looked towards me as I stood at the door, 'how's the hut? Mod. cons. good enough for you?'

'Fine, but I prefer the stars as my ceiling.'

He nodded to my father. 'They don't keep that thing up for long, these young rangers. You know, just now he'll be moaning his hut isn't fitted with an air-conditioner. Come inside, Robbie; isn't that the chief's Land Rover coming up the rise?'

The two dogs had raced outside already.

I came in and sat near my father, unsteadied by an inner lurch as the idea of working for the thundering chief suddenly meshed with reality. Silence now. Sibanda gave me a quick glance, perhaps wondering what mood the chief would be in. Extracting a rhino from a waterhole is not good for one's temper.

Suddenly the silence tumbled under a flood of excited dogs hurtling into the room. Heavy footsteps outside, then, 'So, you made it.' Duma's deep voice seemed untroubled as he appeared in the doorway. Grappling with a rhino didn't seem the kind of thing to draw his thunder. 'Hello Mac, hello Rob.' In a couple of easy strides he had crossed the room and was giving each of us a massive handshake. 'So you didn't wind up in the river after all – where Sibanda said you would. That storm we had yesterday ...'

As I rose, the chief seemed to tower over me. I glanced up at the penetrating eyes set in a face of one who knew about power yet who also knew when not to let it thunder. The rugged, lightly brown features had a look of inner strength that lowered my eyes towards my own shifting feet. Duma's feet were firmly planted and apart. I found myself stupidly wondering what size boots he wore.

'Great to see you both – and Rob, a special welcome to you. Now you're not just a visitor.'

I looked down at the floor again, mumbling something about being glad to be here.

'Sorry I kept you waiting.' He turned towards the fridge. 'Mac, you'll be staying for lunch, won't you?' he asked my father. 'How about something to wash down the dust?'

'Why not indeed?' His soft accent fell gently across the power in Duma's voice. 'A beer would do very nicely.'

'Right.' He held up another can of beer for Sibanda, who nodded. 'And you, Robert?'

'I'd like a beer too, please. How's the rhino?'

'Oh it's all right.' As he handed out the beer he seemed to stare through the wall as if still watching it. 'But what a business to get it out. One of the ropes kept breaking. Cheers!'

He sank fully relaxed in a chair next to my father, legs straight out in front of him, and looked round to where I sat. 'Well Rob, it's good having you here, really good. You seem to be a real maniac about the bush.' The slight grin was mainly to one side of his mouth.

'It seems to be his life,' my father remarked perhaps a little wistfully.

'Eah!' Sibanda pointed at me. 'Let's see how long that lasts. Once a pretty girl visiting camp gets him, she'll make him do something that pays better than being a game ranger. I know what sort of game the girls come to this reserve for – seen it happen too often already.'

Duma started laughing. 'I reckon Banda's not far wrong.' More seriously he said to my father, 'But while he's here, your mission has lost a good worker.'

My father muttered, 'God provides, they say; but not when it comes to staff nowadays.'

Duma put his can thoughtfully to his lips. 'And didn't I say: that's how this century will turn out for the God business?'

'There they go fighting about religion again,' Sibanda said turning to me. 'Always like this, a kind of prize-fight – as if there's nothing better to do in this place than fight the whole time about what or who made it all the way it is.'

'Well,' Duma said, 'there won't be much of that for some time. Did the Game Department tell you, Rob, I'm about to go on leave?'

'Go on leave! I, no, I wasn't expecting ...'

His look was disgruntled as he went to a table just inside the door to pick up some letters placed there.

'Well I suppose there was no real need for them to tell you.' He tossed the letters back in a tray, hardly glancing at them. 'Yes, I'm away for nine whole months.' He didn't sound very excited about it. 'Study leave to finish a book, a book trying to fit together the survival of wildlife and the survival of rural people.'

More gloomily he added, 'Should subtitle the book: A round-up of Africa's problems.'

'Will anyone be taking your place?' I asked.

'Hah!' He had come to life again. 'That sort of thing doesn't happen in this Game Department. The head warden will come round every month or so, and for the rest, the show's got to keep running by itself – and with two new rangers. I'm due to go in four weeks, so you can expect some hectic drilling in that time.'

'Who's the other new ranger?'

Duma looked out of the door as a Land Rover screamed past the house and a moment later we could hear it skidding to a halt near the office.

'Well that's your introduction to him, not out of keeping,' he said. 'Man called Chris Pickerell. Little older than you. Just got his B.Sc., so –' a slightly ironic laugh – 'so he thinks he knows everything. His zoology prof said that young Pickerell is bright but could do with a bit of sobering down. Well, I reckon he's getting it here – appointed to the research staff, but seconded to ranging and he's having a rough time of it.'

That drew a grunt from Sibanda, but I was not sure what it meant.

Duma seemed to understand. 'But he works hard, and he thinks about what he's doing.'

Sibanda shook his head. 'Shall I call him in here? I've got to go and lock the office.'

'I'll go,' Duma said. 'Might be something wrong.'

As the chief left I saw Sibanda roll his eyes upwards as if praying that the 'something wrong' was not of Chris's making. Outside I could hear a conversation being carried on in shouts; when you live in the bush it becomes second nature to speak over distance. Duma's shouts turned to thunder and I could see from Sibanda's face that Chris had run into trouble.

A few moments later Duma was striding through the doorway muttering, 'Bent a mudguard and says he's short of fuel.'

Sibanda shrugged his shoulders. 'I saw him filling up this morning.'

'The way he flies round in that thing,' Duma said, 'it's surprising he doesn't empty his tank in half an hour. Anyway –' the affair seemed to get tossed out of his mind – 'let's have some lunch. You'll have plenty of time, Rob, to meet him when his patrol's finished.'

My father and I stood up while Sibanda went to the door, taking the office keys out of his pocket. At the doorway he stopped, echoing thoughtfully what the chief had said. 'Plenty of time …'

There was a darker shading in his voice as he turned to me. 'You just be careful, Robbie. You be careful that – with all the time here – you don't go fighting with Chris about things your father and the chief always fight about. You know, Robbie …'

His voice dropped a little, as if speaking almost confidentially. 'You know, you get unexpected things happening when people become rangers here. There's that saying, Africa turns people into philosophers or poets. Well, that's not usually true, of course; most people get turned into grabbers and fighters – if they weren't that already. But not all people; not those people who live in and with the real Africa, the Africa that even my own people are growing away from. Yes …'

He turned to look out of the front door, narrowing his eyes as he peered towards the bush spread out in the dazzle and heat. 'Yes, there is something about the bush – its openness, its hugeness – that opens and frightens the mind. When I was in the city, yes, there you were also frightened, but in a different way; there, everything closes your eyes, your mind.'

Hands went to his eyes. 'You are blind. But, a few of us, we come here, and –' his hands suddenly splayed open in front of his face – 'Hau! Your eyes, they open; your mind, it sees, somehow it wakes; it wakes up in a new way. Then, you find yourself starting to ask questions, new questions – questions so new they scare you.' Arms opened out wide, '*big* questions, and you become a philosopher – of a sort, anyway. The trouble is …'

He looked back at me again. 'The trouble is, Robbie, people can become kind of bush-mad. They think and they talk and they think and they fight the whole time; fight about who or what made this place the way it is. Bush-mad! That's what I call it. Bush-mad. And now, Robbie …'

A finger was being shaken at me in warning. 'From what I know of Chris – and you – if you two start fighting the way the chief and your father keep on fighting; well, you know, with the chief going away now, I don't want to have to go round picking up pieces that you and Chris leave everywhere. Just be careful, Robbie, see?'

Duma's glance at me had an air of sizing something up, but he didn't say anything.

Chapter Two

After lunch, outside the office in the bright blazing sun, my father had little to say as he climbed into the mission Land Rover. His look had a touch of defeat as he drove off alone. The wrench I felt was unexpectedly strong: 'Have I let him down really badly?' I muttered to myself as I watched him clear the camp gates, my last wave to him cut short by Sibanda calling from inside the office.

'Hey, Robbie; quartermaster's parade or what you call it.'

He pointed at a heap of khaki clothing on the office desk, my Game Department uniform. 'This uniform – it makes you a target for a poacher's bullet, this stuff.'

I took 'this stuff' to my hut, and began changing. A ranger's uniform; how I had expected a sense of achievement the first time I put it on. Yet, matched against the final look my father gave me, something now seemed lacking. And how would I shape against the other rangers? Put on a ranger's uniform and you are a target for more than just a poacher. How would I look in the eyes of the people working here?

There was a knock on the door.

'Come in.'

Silence, then more knocking.

'Come in!'

Further silence, followed by more knocking.

I tied a final knot in my boots and went to open the door.

'Shine your shoes, sir?' The face that peered in had a clownish look, even more funny since beneath the expression were strikingly good, rather eagle-like features. Light, wavy hair gave a crispness to the whole effect, even though the uniform shirt was half hanging out.

'Oh, you must be Chris Pickerell.'

‘Right. Robert McBraid, I presume.’ He drew himself up and bowed stiffly, doffing an imaginary pith helmet.

We laughed and shook hands.

‘So, won’t you come in now?’

‘Not with the boss out there. He wants me to show you the guard posts. So put away your bottle of gin like a good boy, and let’s go.’

Behind him was a Land Rover left revving as if ready for take-off. As I followed him and clambered into the passenger’s seat I began to see why Chris’s zoology professor felt he could do with a bit of sobering.

‘Hell, you’re lucky you didn’t come here yesterday,’ he shouted as we hurtled out of the camp gates. ‘See that mud wallow over there? That’s where that bloody rhino got stuck last night. Would’ve been eaten alive by hyaenas if we’d left it – you could see from the spoor that they tried making a breakfast of it early this morning.’

‘Not too good for the rhino,’ I said clutching my seat as Chris swung off the road past the wallow.

‘Not too good for the tourists,’ he replied sharply, bouncing back onto the road. ‘God, can you imagine the squeal they’d’ve made? “Poor rhino, how could you let a thing like that happen?” – as if that kind of thing isn’t happening in the bush the whole time anyway.’

He accelerated even more. ‘Either that, or they’d’ve caused a traffic jam round the place to have a look, like people crowding round a road smash. The bloodier the better. The things people do in this reserve – what made you want to be a ranger here?’

‘Well, a lot of reasons. I suppose you can say I have a mad interest all round.’

My eyes were on the speedometer needle climbing into the sixties. I wondered what would happen if we met a tourist car round the next bend.

'Mad interest?' Chris raised his eyebrows half sympathetically, half cynically. 'Hell, then I feel sorry for you.'

'Why?'

'Because – well, most guys seem to join the Game Department because they've got romantic ideas about being out in the bush and being tough, wearing a uniform and driving round in a bush-cart like this. Well, they just get what's coming to them: stupid administration, stupid tourists, stupid game. But guys who join because they want to be intelligent about things and actually do something interesting – they're the ones who get messed up.'

'How come?'

'First, you're up against the bone-headed collection of people in administration who have no idea of this place except as a kind of market commodity. Second, you soon find you have to spend all your time being driven nuts either by poachers or by tourists – in the end you don't know which wreck the place most, either shooting it out or flattening it out with off-road driving. Well, put those two things together and how can you do anything intelligent in this place? Can't even call it a game reserve – it's just part of the tourist track, there for the money; stuff the game.'

'The chief said that actually you were appointed to the research staff, not the ranging staff; but all that happened was ...'

'Right.' He rounded the bend with a quick swerve to avoid some zebra before hurtling along the track again. 'All that happened was – the old story: the administration suddenly finds it hasn't got the money or the time to keep a mere scientist in business. And so – "Just for half a year, would you mind being on the ranging staff?" Well, after a month I've just about reached the point where I *do* mind. This might be a fantastic place for scientific research, but God, you try and actually run it.'

His interest switched to a slow-moving vortex of vultures on his side of the track. 'Let's see what's cooking over there,' he said as he pointed out of the window.

Without slowing down he swung the Land Rover off the track and rocketed through the bush, just skirting the larger trees and brushing over saplings.

'Hold everything!' he shouted.

The advice was hardly necessary – I was doing all I could to keep near my seat.

'The funny thing is that the chief says I drive like a cowboy,' he gleefully added, reeling round an antbear hole.

Before I could remind him about tourists flattening the place by off-road driving, we pulled up at the remains of a kill. Scrambled beneath the vultures were bits of a wildebeest.

He peered through his window to look for spoor. 'Wonder whodunit,' he said.

We climbed out, Chris with a machete in his hand, beating away some vultures with its flat blade.

He gave the twisted ropes of skin and bone a cursory glance, then lifted his machete. With one stroke he chopped open the snout, exposing a mass of wriggling maggots.

'Ever seen those nasal maggots before? A fly enters the nostrils and lays its eggs there.'

Idly he tapped the skull with the blade and some maggots rolled out on the hot sand. They wriggled. He looked abstractedly at the white, writhing mass for a moment before scooping it all back into the skull.

'Makes you sick, sometimes,' he said.

The stench alone could make you feel that. He stood up to get away from it, looking casually at lion spoor all round the carcass before sauntering back to the Land Rover, kicking a dislodged leg ahead of him.

We climbed aboard without a word, apart from Chris saying in mock officialise as he opened a notebook, 'Come on Pickerell, record everything you observe. No promotion otherwise.'

Once again we started off for the guard post.

But as I was finding, Chris is not the kind of person to keep quiet for long.

'I reckon most people don't know what problems are until they start working here,' he said as we raced along the track. 'It's one thing to be a starry-eyed visitor going round gawping at everything. But when you work here, trying to keep it all together, then you see what a shambles the set-up really is.'

'How d'you mean?'

'Talk about problems – if you don't have enough lion in the reserve to keep the number of grazers down, the place gets grazed flat; and if you do have enough lion they take to marauding outside the reserve, and you have the police and the politicians coming down on your head. Mindless opportunism, that's what this set-up works on – and as a ranger you have to keep the whole thing from imploding.'

'It doesn't always have to seem mindless like that.'

Eyebrows rose questioningly. 'Well what else can it seem?'

At the mission I would have had a ready answer. A witness to the living God; or as dwellers round the mission saw it, the work of the Great Creator. To them there was nothing mindless about what went on in the bush. Seeing the bush as mindless was white man's madness, a measure of the white man's alienation from nature. But, 'Just be careful, Robbie.' Sibanda's warning was coming back to me; 'Don't go fighting with Chris about things the chief and your father always fight about.'

So I shrugged my shoulders and said nothing.

Luckily we were drawing into the western guard post, a miniature enclave of three huts and a store-room tucked away in the bush. While I had been just a visitor the guard posts were not my business, but now I had to see them as key areas.

‘Slept in this place the night before last,’ Chris said as he pushed open a hut door. ‘Didn’t realize till half-way through the night that I was sharing the hut with a bloody cobra.’

‘What were you doing here?’

He put on a mock-officious bearing again. ‘You might as well know, McBraid, that these guard posts are not just here for your recreation.’ Even more stuffily: ‘As local bases in our relentless campaign against poaching, it will be your duty to … rats!’

He slammed the hut door and went back to the Land Rover.

‘All we did on that little trip was bring back a game guard with his chest blown open by someone out for rhino.’

He started with a roar and swung round onto another track heading for a post near the northern gate.

Almost no streams run in the northern, sandy area. We hurtled through a mixture of brittle grass and scrub, the game sheltering from heat among scattered thickets – and just as well, I thought; any animal suddenly darting across the track would have us in trouble.

‘So.’ Chris screwed his nose a little as he leaned back in his seat, arms having to stretch out to reach the steering-wheel. ‘The chief told you about my being appointed to the research staff, and then being switched to ranging.’

‘Yes.’

‘And what else did he say happens to people who get signed up here?’

‘Nothing much. All I know is that he’s going to give me a tough time; all the drilling before he leaves in four weeks.’

‘Do you know much about this place; I mean, did you come visiting here before you signed up?’

‘My folks and I came once a year, and I made it more often – whenever I could. Did … did the chief say anything to you about what I was doing before I came here? Estate manager?’

'Well, let's face it, the chief hasn't said much because he knows I'm not exactly spellbound by what might go on at a mission.'

'Not quite your kind of scene?'

A drawn face and upward roll of the eyes showed definitely it was not. 'Went to a church school and that was more than enough for me. All the stuff rammed down your throat – talk about overkill.'

Racing through the dense scrub, I wondered what else was liable to suffer overkill. He was hardly glancing at the winding track as he launched into what seemed a favourite theme: 'How can you take on board the Biblical stuff like … how does it go? "Be fruitful and multiply, subdue the earth." And once you've subdued the earth? Then what d'you do?'

Both hands were off the steering wheel, waving about. 'Starve! That's all that can happen; starve, with a collapsed environment around you.'

He turned round to me as if expecting a response. But Sibanda's warning was with me again: 'You just be careful, Robbie …'

I said nothing.

Chris was having to slow down for an ostrich and a cluster of chicks scurrying across the road.

'Fruitful multipliers,' he muttered pointing to the chicks as they scrambled off the roadside into a thicket. 'Those little guys will nearly all end up in carnivores' stomachs, and that's how things get controlled here; but *people* …' He picked up speed again. 'Why does the Church think we can get away with being fruitful multipliers without any need of control? Yet you see them coming round here telling us that God gave man dominion over nature – and then they make off with the pickings.'

I was about to reply, 'I *don't* go round saying that … at least, I don't even if half the mission does.' But I looked back at the road again with Sibanda's warning sounding once more.

So again I did not say anything. But I could not help thinking back to Sibanda's remark about picking up pieces if Chris and I ever got stuck into each other. Whose pieces would he have to pick up? I wondered

Chapter Three

How many different hues of green can you count in the bush on a fresh, dew-drenched morning?

What an impossible question! At sunrise on the first full day of my new career I was up, excited and expectant. Yes, a real maniac about the bush – isn't that what the chief himself had said of me?

The morning brightness would be at its glistening best down at the riverside pans. Maybe some tourists would have the same idea, and I would be able to take along a party.

But a walk among the huts showed no sign of life in the camp. No sign at least until I came across Duma standing by himself near the office, feet slightly apart, hands on hips, looking intently into the lightening sky.

'Brought rain with you?' he asked as I drew close.

'Well you had quite a good preview of my rain-making the day before yesterday.'

He grunted. 'In this place you wait months for rain; then when it comes you have to spend months clearing up the mess afterwards. I want you to check the bridge, Rob. It didn't ditch your father's Land Rover yesterday, but there's no knowing what it'll do to the next car that goes over it, and the maintenance team is busy with other flood damage.'

After a quick breakfast, with the sun already high and burning, I set out to the bridge. Packed in the truck with a heap of tools was a feeling of terrific importance. My first assignment; I was going through the reserve not as a wide-eyed tourist, or even a serious biologist. I had essential work to do. The game that I passed received hardly more than a patronizing glance.

Little needed to be done to the bridge. A thickset span of timber, massive beams held in concrete from sandy bank to bank – it would take a tsunami to bring down something like this. In the coolness of towering sycamore figs that lined the bank it was tempting to spend the whole day there. A few cars rumbled across the bridge, but at noon as I was finishing off, a convoy of three cars stopped right in the middle. I climbed the river bank to the road. The last car had rammed into the side railings, and someone – I suppose about my age – was leaning out of the driver's window. I could see a pale, gaunt face with pitch black hair hanging down one side of the forehead; his look seemed slightly glazed as he stared at the wooden railing wedged against the car.

His head turned languidly round as he saw me. 'I saaay.' It was a slurred parody of a classy accent. 'Do tell me, where do you keep your dinosaurs?'

The question was celebrated by cheers from the rest of the people in the car.

I put on an equally phoney drawl. 'They be yonder, by them thar hills.'

Another round of cheers, and I started to wonder what had got into them. Not merely delights of the African wilds.

'For Pete's sake,' I said, 'where have you people come from?'

A girl stuck her head out of the window. 'We come from haunt of coot and hern,' she warbled.

Someone shouted from the car in front. 'It's all right. It's just them. We haven't started ours yet.'

'Started what?'

'Stuff we bought at the roadside, just outside the reserve gates.'

The gaunt face in the last car volunteered, 'Boosting the local economy. Benefits of tourism and all that.'

I walked up to the second car. 'What the hell are they talking about?'

A little uneasily, the driver half got out of the car to explain. They had seen the cut stumps of palm trees, with tin cans hanging below the oozing ends to collect sap. 'We stopped to ask a group of people ...'

He was interrupted by the girl in the last car, still leaning out of her window. 'We bought bowls –' she held a clay pot unsteadily out of the window – 'bowls from a couple of women at the roadside.'

'Four of them,' said the gaunt face.

'No,' the girl insisted, 'there were two; two of them.'

'Not the women – the pots. Four pots of palm wine.'

The driver of the second car muttered, 'This is a student club – if you haven't guessed that already. The last car is full of drama students. Their pots began leaking so they've started drinking already.'

I asked, 'Are you heading for camp?'

'The two front cars are. God knows where that one –' he pointed to the last car – 'is heading.'

'To mate with the crocodiles in the river, it seems. Don't you have a spare driver to take them home?'

Someone else shouted from the middle car, 'I'll drive.'

'Then unless you want the contents of the last car to be distributed among those crocodiles, you'd better take over.'

'Oh.' The gaunt face in the last car had resumed a slurred toff accent. 'What a perfectly splendid idea.'

Someone emerged from the middle car to take over the driving. He had a slightly sheepish look. 'We're supposed to be clocking in for a couple of nights, if we can make it to base.'

'Well, go easy on that palm wine. It's lethal stuff.'

With a 'So it seems,' he took over the wheel, and the convoy rumbled off the bridge on its way to the main camp.

There seemed nothing wrong with the bridge if it had held three cars, one half ramming it. So after fixing the railing I packed my goods and followed them.

'Funny people you get coming here,' I remarked to Duma as I reported at the office.

He merely grunted 'Students' and put me onto studying ordinances; legal aspects of wildlife protection, a tangle of print that seemed specially designed to make the prosecution of a poacher impossible unless caught actually de-gutting his quarry. For the rest of the afternoon Duma came in and out of the office muttering about what had to be done before he left.

A few people from the student party came in to buy picture postcards. One end of the office had been turned into a curio shop, but most of the goods there were too expensive for them.

'Where's Chris?' an older looking student asked me. They were all from the same university, he said. 'That's one reason why we're here, to see if he's wrecked the place yet.'

'He's out on patrol. How are the drama people in the last car doing?'

'Flat on their backs.'

It was sundown by this time. As Duma came in, 'For pity's sake,' I said to him. 'I'll be looking like a lawyer's clerk if I go on like this.'

'A lawyer's clerk?' It was the first time I had seen him amused all afternoon. 'That's one of the things you're supposed to be. All right, Rob.' He signalled to my hut. 'Get your things for a short break at the river. After that, how about a bite at my place?'

My reply became drowned by shouting outside the office as a patrol car drove up. Was a student car in trouble again? I wondered.

Duma went to the door.

'He nearly killed us!' The noise came from game guards as they jumped out of the vehicle and shouted in the vividness of their Zulu.

'Back wheel bitten off ...'

'We had to walk ...'

'Hau! Hau!' Duma left the office to meet Makanya storming across to him. 'Makanya,' he called out in Zulu, 'what is it?'

'That young ranger of yours, Sharp-faced One, him, he has smashed a patrol car, made it skid into a tree.'

I glanced round to see where Chris was as Duma asked, 'Anyone hurt?'

'Three of my guards were with him. It was only their ancestral spirits that saved them from getting hurt.'

'And Sharp-faced One?'

Makanya waved angrily towards Chris's hut. 'He has gone, there, like a bruised monkey.'

At least, I thought, it wasn't the student party that had started the fuss. Duma turned to me. 'Go and see how Chris is, Robert. I'll take Makanya's men back to their guard camp. We can see about the patrol Rover tomorrow.'

A light was showing in Chris's hut, so I walked across, thinking he had gone into retreat there.

As I looked through the door I heard a terse 'All right, officer, I'll come quietly.'

He lay sprawled on his bed, rubbing an elbow. 'How did the chief take it?'

'Pretty calmly.'

'It's at times like this when I – God, I wish he'd bloody well take off when this kind of thing happens. Then at least you'd get it over.'

'Somehow I wouldn't like to be at the receiving end when he does take off.'

'I dunno. It's worse when he makes you feel a tit all next day. Anyway, there's nothing wrong with the bush-cart really – just a back fender jammed against the wheel.'

'How did you do it?'

'Porcupine ran across the road and I swerved – at least, that's my story. Actually that's what happened. The guards saw it all.'

'Bet they did. Wide-eyed. How fast were you going?'

'Oh well, what's sixty k's an hour between friends? I'd just about stopped skidding by the time I hit the tree, anyway. Bugger it, it was the only big tree in the whole bloody area. I suppose that's part of your divine justice.'

I laughed. 'Well, only naughty boys drive at sixty in a game reserve.'

'All right. I'll be hearing enough about that from the chief. Let's have grub with those students – or maybe I should save up for my condemned man's breakfast tomorrow.'

'Actually, the chief asked me across for supper tonight.'

'Well I don't know what time you'll get it after this little flurry. Wasn't that the chief's Land Rover going out again? Suppose he's gone to call the police to arrest me.'

'I think I'll go and ask Sibanda if the chief said anything to him about supper.'

I went over to Sibanda's house – the office lights were out by this time – and knocked on his door.

'Hello Robbie.' Sibanda came to the door with a beer in his hand. 'Come along in.'

'Oh, I was just going to ask if the chief said anything about supper tonight.'

'Yes, he said: don't wait for him. Have something with us if you're not lined up already.'

'Seems that the student party want to line up something with Chris and me. I suppose Chris should make the best of it before he gets lined up tomorrow in front of the chief.'

'Chris? Man, he should be sent to bed without any supper. Anyway, you go, Robbie. See you tomorrow.'

Chapter Four

'What a crazy lot.'

I found Chris leaning against his hut door, hands in pockets, scanning the party with a casually superior look. They were milling about at the edge of the tourist area, about twelve of them, picked up and lost again like midges in the light from hut windows and open doors. And what a noise: shouting, singing, car doors slamming.

'I'm not going to kill myself with their palm wine,' Chris said. 'But …' he started to move across to them, 'we could feed one or two of them to the hyaenas – kind of low-key Roman holiday.'

As we came close we heard 'Hey, Chris!' shouted by an eager face lit up outside a hut window. A huge pair of spectacles was skewed on the nose. 'Fantastic health drink – have some.'

'That stuff?' Chris asked. 'You've never heard what palm wine can do?'

'We're busy finding that out,' someone else shouted through a window we were standing beside. 'What's the alcohol content supposed to be?'

'Depends how long it's been fermenting,' Chris said. 'You only know how much alcohol there is by sampling it: biological assay – seeing how badly it socks you.'

'Wow!' The guy with the skewed specs had certainly been socked.

I asked, 'What's happened to the lot in your last car on the bridge?'

The spectacles turned my way. 'How do I know? Those of us who were still functioning took that stuff down to the hippo pool at the river. Jeez, we only just made it back to camp – gates were being closed for the night as we came round the home bend. We're still …'

One of several girls with the almost uniform long hair, tee-shirt and jeans had come running up to where we stood, hands fluttering round her face in panic. I recognized her; in the drama students' car she was the one leaning out of a window with a pot of wine.

'Steve, Steve.'

The spectacles were unsteadily pivoted round to her.

'Steve, Craig isn't here. He's – did you see him come back with us? I mean …' She gave Chris and me a wide-eyed look, a mixture of guilt and alarm. A hand brushed loose strands of blonde hair from her face. 'I mean, when we all got out to wee at the hippo pool, did … did we all get back into cars again?'

'Search me, Cheryl.' Steve blinked helplessly behind his glasses, looking uneasily at us. This was a leak of incriminating information; no-one is allowed out of a car unless at a protected place, and there is nothing like that at the hippo pool. 'But …' Now Steve was looking puzzled. 'You should know about Craig, Cheryl.'

She pouted. 'He was sharing his pot of wine with Jenny, so – well I didn't care *whose* car he was in.' Clenched hands went to her mouth, agonizingly.

'Craig is Cheryl's boyfriend,' Steve murmured to us, adding more glumly, 'as if that information's going to help. What …' now his look had become worried. 'What do we do?'

'I reckon,' Chris said drily, 'the first thing you do is have another look to make sure he really didn't come back with you. Hell, were you all so stoned that …'

Steve was scratching his head. 'We were pretty high on that palm wine by the time we got moving to camp. All three cars and …' He paused with the earnest look of an intellectual diamond-runner who was coming clean. 'You see, we didn't *only* get out of the cars at the pool. We kept getting out all the way back. And we didn't all come back along the same road. One car came back along the road on the other side of the river – we kept shouting to each other across the river, like, mind the lions and things.'

'Ooh!' Cheryl turned, hands still clasped in front of her mouth as she ran back to the milling crowd around the huts. Light hair tossing wildly behind her, in a couple of seconds she had vanished among the chaos.

'What a set-up,' Chris said. 'And the chief's gone to take those game guards home.'

'And we're short of a Land Rover,' I remarked, thinking of what Chris had abandoned with a smashed wheel out in the bush.

'I'll take the truck,' Chris replied huffily. 'Steve, you'd better come with me to show where you stopped along the way. Rob, you get the other patrol Rover and –' he marched off with Steve as a kind of hostage – 'rake up someone else to go with you along the other side of the river.'

'Okay.'

I began making my way towards the remaining patrol Rover past the palm wine festival. In the lights I could see the guy with the gaunt face, almost doubled up, hand against a tree near the parking lot. Probably just thrown up; black hair stood out starkly against the ashen colour.

'You all right?' I asked, wondering how stupid the question sounded.

Very stupid, judging from the look he gave. 'God, I just wish I'd been left out in the bush to be eaten by the hyaenas,' he groaned.

'Did you go to the hippo pool?'

He nodded weakly.

'Haven't you heard? One of your crowd really *has* been left out. When you were all crawling out of your cars, seems that someone didn't get back fast enough – got caught with his pants down, so to speak.'

'Doesn't surprise me,' he said weakly. 'That palm wine …'

'Can you remember which road you took coming back? The one this side of the river, or the other side?'

'Other side.'

'Well that's the one I'm supposed to be going out to check. D'you remember where you stopped on the way back?'

'Do I remember? That's where I first …' He put a hand grimly across his stomach. 'A kind of cliff at the edge of the road. I was thinking, well at least a lion isn't going to grab me here; you can hurl a cat over the cliff without a lion flying up at you.'

'Then d'you feel like coming with me, to look for a guy who might've been left there?'

His drooping head turned towards a bunch who were prancing round at the edge of the tourist huts. 'God, just look at that lot,' he muttered. '*Homo sapiens,* man the wise, that's what they call our species. Bloody idiots. There's no way I'm going back for more of that palm wine stuff.'

The drawn face turned to me. 'I'll go with you, back to the sanity of the monkeys and baboons out there.'

In a short while I was driving the second patrol Rover out of the gate and down the winding road to the river. My passenger – he had mumbled his name but I didn't catch it – was grimly silent. He sat hunched in his seat, but yes, he could remember which way they'd come: there, across the reed-lined river, over a concrete causeway covered by five centimetres of fast-flowing water. 'Thought the guy driving the car was going to go over the edge, right into the drink – nearly passed out.'

Once over the causeway I drove slowly along the riverside road, main beams on and engine revving noisily in low gear to alert whoever might be missing.

Then the stretch of road above the cliff – my passenger spoke tensely as he pointed that out to me, sounding as though there was still more in the pipeline to come up. Yet we saw no frantic figure waving us down at the roadside; no sign of human life, in fact, until we reached the hippo pool and saw across the inky water the lights of Chris's truck shining from the parking area on the opposite bank.

Above the rattling chorus of toads at either edge of the river, 'Not found anyone?' we shouted almost simultaneously to each other.

There was no need for a reply. All Chris did was fling a comment out of his truck window, 'Stuff the whole stupid thing, anyway.'

He started his truck and we watched it pull off until it disappeared behind a dense screen of reeds.

'Might as well go back too,' I said turning to my passenger as I wondered dimly why the Rover was rocking slightly. The reason was simple: palm wine can be merciless, especially when fortified by all the insects that fall into the tins and get brewed up with it. As he leaned his head out of the cab window the best I could do was hand him a flask of water.

'Made a hell of a mess down the side of the car,' he croaked as he pulled his head in.

'Not to worry. It can be hosed down when we get back to camp.'

'*If* we get back to camp,' he muttered. 'I reckon, just dig a hole somewhere here, dump me in it and carve on the nearest tree: Here lies Craig Taylor, the man who …'

He stopped, surprised, as he saw me suddenly sit bolt upright in my seat.

'Craig? Craig? Hey, do you have a girlfriend called Cheryl?'

In his strangled voice there was a touch of fire. 'Cheryl? Yes. What's it … what's it got to do with you?'

'Ohh, no.' I put my hand to my forehead. 'Hell's delight, we'd better get right back to camp, quickly.'

'Hey? If it's anything to do between you and Cheryl, then –' the bull in high blood – 'I want to know about it *now*. Right now.'

'What? Me and …? Wait a minute; we're getting into one hell of a …'

I stopped, taken aback by another slight rocking of the Rover and a strange rasping sound coming from Craig's side of the cab. I saw him peer out of the open window. A second later he flung himself back with something close to a scream.

'What's up?' I shouted.

His mouth was open in a terror that made his whole body rigid as he leaned away from the window. I scrambled over him to look out. Two lionesses, they were sitting at the edge of the road watching us indifferently. And – craning a bit more out of the window – I could see a full-maned lion standing up against the door. Gently I pulled the window closed as: rasp, rasp, rasp. He was idly licking Craig's offering off the side of the cab door.

I put my hand to the keys to switch on the ignition, but noise and lights from another vehicle suddenly broke up the party, a Land Rover heading in the direction of camp. It pulled up beside us and I had a half second to start adding up how much trouble I was in.

'What the hell's happening out here?' I could hear Duma thunder. He was on his way back from taking the guards home.

What was the use of trying to explain it all?

'We're just some *Homo sapienses* feeding the lions,' I said weakly.

The expression on the chief's face, picked in the reflected light from the vehicles, needed no interpretation: a second ranger was being been lined up for a condemned man's breakfast.

Not a very good start of a career, I thought as he drove off.

That night I did not sleep well.

Chapter Five

Sunrise on my second day took me round the camp, like the first day thinking there might be tourists interested in visiting the riverside pans at bird-song. Perhaps I could do better than last night's trip, I thought. I saw Duma standing outside the office, hands shielding eyes against the growing sunlight, staring into the sky. I approached him wondering what thunder he had lined up for me.

He surveyed me as I stood droopily before him. Then, 'Rob, don't be as big a tit as Chris can sometimes be,' was all he had to say. He gave the sky another glance. 'Maybe a storm later. Coming down to the pans?'

The cock-up seemed thrown out of his mind, yet I still felt an idiot as we climbed into his Land Rover. My first outing with the chief as a ranger; if last night's fiasco was not weighing on me I'd have been perched excitedly on the edge of my seat during the trip down to the floodplain, pointing even at the commonest sight of dark-and-light speckled hornbills waddling along the roadside, snatching insects with huge yellow beaks. Life and light was all around us, but I only started to feel it as we passed the first fever-trees; we were reaching the floodplain.

Duma drove slowly, elbow resting as usual on the window ledge. He would silently point to some animal standing concealed in the bush, one that few would be likely to spot. For him a drive through the bush was a study, an observational exercise. He never encouraged talking, yet, 'And here it all is,' I found myself saying in wonder as we arrived at the largest pan. Bright sparkle of morning light carried my glance across the water to the other side, a shimmering half-kilometre away, then up and down the length of the pan, too long to make out its ends except for distant reeds.

Water-lilies spread in sheets over the finely-flashing surface, probing the air with sky-blue flowers and damping the brilliance of the pan with rounded, flat green pads. Sandy beaches, coves and water inlets made breaks in the line of slender reeds, and beyond them lawns of close-cropped grass reached under the shade of fever-trees until stopped by the rugged bush around us.

For a while Duma followed a track skirting the water's edge, then drew up under a towering fever-tree, its yellowy-green trunk throwing up tracery, green and brilliant, into the blueness of sky. Here at the water's edge we climbed out.

The scene seldom fails to envelop its spectators. When your eyes have taken their fill of the placid water, broken here and there by the swirl of fish or perhaps by a lazing crocodile, then look up and scan the greeny-yellow fever-trees for a great dark and white fish-eagle perched high on a branch. Watch it for a while, and it will throw back its head and yodel its call. There is no mistaking it – it is the authentic and exultant cry of the African wilds.

So many other birds are calling that the different sounds can hardly be told apart; but through it you can hear the hippos, returned from a night of foraging on land. Little more than their leathery snouts, eyes and flicking ears are above water, but you can easily pick them out as they join in a round of honking bellows and grunts. Now and again one of them opens its jaws in a massive yawn.

One must have time to absorb this wonder, the feel of stillness behind all the honks and calls, since it cannot be grasped all at once. And in this bird-sung stillness Duma and I left the Land Rover to make our way along the pan's edge towards his favourite look-out spot, a natural hide formed by a little reed-lined spit pointing into the gently rippling water. Here we sat and absorbed our surroundings.

Yet one part of what we absorbed could well have been left out. There was a smell of something very dead. I looked round the lapping edge of water, and in the reeds. Nothing there. Also nothing where we sat. I glanced behind us. Something furry hung in a small fever-tree about a metre from the ground. And for the first time I noticed all the trees at that level carried a high-water mark of debris.

I pointed to the mute catastrophe of litter. 'Is all that from the storm?'

Duma did not even trouble to look behind him. 'Quite a lot of game gets drowned whenever this pan's flooded.'

He screwed his face slightly. 'It's not one of the best things to see.'

There was silence again. Silence and the smell. Bits of the first afternoon's trip with Chris began to flicker through my brain, and I murmured, 'Chris said, when you start working here you begin to realize what a shambles this whole set-up really is. He sounded … somehow alienated from the bush. To him the bush seemed a kind of mindless machine – an almost senseless machine, and our job here was to, to sort of cope with it like a mangled piece of clockwork.'

Duma turned to me. 'And what do you think of that?'

'I know what people living round the mission think. They'd think: white man's blindness, the idea of nature being some mindless, senseless machine. Nature to them is alive, creative, filled with spirit; frightening, sometimes – very frightening, but not just a machine.'

Duma repeated, 'And what do *you* –' he pointed at me for emphasis – 'think?'

'Of Chris's idea? I'd call it alienated, materialistic, mechanistic madness. That simply is not how the living bush can strike a truly aware person, just a thing that's ultimately dead. The bush then becomes a – what? – an unfeeling abstraction, something you just make theories about and mechanically "manage" according to your theories. To me that's uncaring, uncomprehending. If I ever came round to believing what Chris thinks, then … something inside me would have to die.'

Duma made no comment. So I turned his question on him. 'What do *you* think?'

He looked at the ground for a moment as though he had to make a decision. Then he said, 'I think we can leave that, Robert, for the time being anyway. What you or I make of it is something that can wait till you've been here longer.'

But – whether disturbed by the smell or not I wasn't sure – he rose fairly deliberately, standing high among the reeds, and lifted his field-glasses for a quick scan about him before making his way back to the Land Rover.

I followed a bit self-consciously, feeling I had spoiled something – at least for myself – by what I had just been talking about. At the edge of the pan I paused and watched him climb into the cab, my attention half diverted by yesterday's exchange with Chris still bobbing about in my head. And, 'You know, Robbie.' Sibanda's voice was sounding again; 'You get unexpected things happening when people become rangers here.'

Nonsense. Duma and I had different views, of course. But they had not been a problem in the past, so why should they matter now? I gave myself a shake; a quick haul and I was in the Land Rover, shutting the door beside me. A glance out of the window showed plenty of game approaching the water; all sorts of buck, some zebra, all cautiously moving towards the water's edge. That's why we were in the cab, of course. The game would stay under cover as long as we were knocking about out there.

'You know, Robbie, you get unexpected things…'

I half glanced at Duma. He was writing something in his field book, silent and impassive. That's how he often was, of course; but why did I feel a sting of irritation, almost resentfulness? Was it the way he'd said, 'What you or I make of it is something that can wait till you've been here longer'? As if I wasn't yet ready to take something on?

Chuck it, I thought as I gave myself another shake; I'm not the kind of person to go bush-mad, as Sibanda called it, arguing the whole time about what or who made this place the way it is.

'Gosh, what a sight,' I said turning to look out of the window at the game now reaching the pan's edge. But I knew the remark sounded flat.

All it drew from Duma was a grunt, and I could not make out what it meant.

He started the engine, and without saying any more we arrived at camp for breakfast.

Chapter Six

After breakfast the chief put me back on the ordinances, saying he was going to quiz me about them in two hour's time. But by two hours I saw him standing at the office door. A towering storm cloud was developing south of the reserve; its dark grey-green colour and heavy pocketing made him look uneasy, work forgotten as he wondered if it would burst over the reserve.

'See that?' he said as I joined him. 'There's hail in that cloud.'

The swirling base was quickly expanding and darkening; the billowing white mass above erupted and heaved mountain upon mountain above the plain. Lightning darted and flashed incessantly, making a continuous roar of thunder. In a few more minutes the grey-black savage base crashed to earth, rain and hail pelting the land.

The dark wall spread and we could see that the south-eastern corner of the reserve did not escape the battering.

Duma looked grim. 'Come on, Robert, we'd better get out there. Bring a rifle.'

The last order surprised me, but I hurried into the office for a rifle and clambered into Duma's Land Rover as it was drawing away.

By the time we reached the south-east sector the storm had already passed. Left behind it was a motionless, shattered piece of country, heavy with the smell of ripped vegetation and stilled in an eerie, almost painful silence. No birds, no sounds at all. Hailstones not much smaller than a fist lay in great drifts over the ground, condensing a strange white fog as if a pall were being formed to cover the hushed and lifeless bush.

Yet not completely lifeless – even worse; as we started slithering along the hail-swept track, something lying to one side under a de-leafed tree made us stop. A crowned eagle, one of our most treasured birds, lay struggling to right itself. It looked horribly injured, as if it had been bombed clean out of the sky by hail.

Duma climbed out of the Land Rover. I was unable to move, numbed by the appalling sadness of what was here. This king of the skies, its future now only slow death and the hyaenas. After examining it, Duma wordlessly returned to the cab and pulled out a rifle. Now I could see why I had been told to bring one too. There would be more casualties like this, so many more that shooting was the only kind way to deal with them.

Duma's single comment as he stowed his rifle back into the cab was, 'Some people say, let nature take its course, let battered animals go gangrenous, let them get eaten alive by hyaenas; that's nature. I say: things here have been punished enough already.'

The survey of storm damage kept us busy till nightfall. Nsundu and Chris had joined, and by the time we returned to our Land Rovers Chris was the only one who had anything to say. But even he had lost his jauntiness.

He muttered to me, 'If there really is a god of yours who did all this, then he's a total *bastard.*'

Certainly I was in no mood for comments as we clambered into our vehicles to return through the night-shrouded bush, through this world of nature I had been brought up to believe was the work of a divine, benevolent Intelligence.

'There is something about the bush …' Sibanda's warning was rumbling ominously like a thunder-cloud; 'something about the bush that opens and frightens the mind. You find yourself starting to ask questions, questions so new they scare you.' Like, what's the good of setting up a whole lot of ordinances when the divine hand can destroy more in half an hour than a gang of poachers could in ten years?

But I knew the bush well enough from my time at the mission, managing my own reserve. No need to worry about questions. Acts of God – fire, flood and famine – that isn't news to anyone familiar with the wilds. Nothing there to question the assurances of all the books in my father's study.

Yet – only now it really struck me – looking after a small nature reserve on a mission is not the same as this. In a small reserve, you can do something about distressed animals; it can be a part of the management. There, only the remnants of the wilds survived, a handful of animals left over from man's destructiveness; and no hyaenas, no lion. But here, in the wilds – the real wilds, unimaginably vast and merciless – here there is not man's destructiveness but the destructiveness of God. Acts of God; what sort of omnipotent Creator would plan out his works in this gruesome way? And now, was it really my job to protect these works against this Creator? As a ranger, was I to rescue creation against the acts of its Creator? Was I to defy this Creator; or merely judge him simply to be inept?

'Most people,' Chris had said on our first afternoon out, 'don't know what problems are until they start working here.'

I had not felt responsible for the wilds before; and that made an unexpected difference between being a mission estate manager and being a game ranger.

'You find yourself starting to ask questions,' Sibanda had said. 'Questions so new they scare you.'

The next day I was stuck in the office once more, working through ordinances. Duma told me I would not be allowed out of the office until he was satisfied I knew them.

'Now you know what being a ranger is like,' Chris remarked as he surveyed me through a window. 'You spend more time driving a desk than a Land Rover.'

The sun came burning through the open door, then dropped towards the horizon leaving the office dull and bleak. It matched a feeling growing inside me as the afternoon wore on. A storm rumbled far to the east, dropping its deadly load outside the reserve. Pictures of yesterday's hailstorm started to batter into my thoughts: what sense is there in learning the legalities of game protection when God in his heaven can break every regulation in the book?

Late in the afternoon the student party came to the office looking for more postcards. The drama students of Craig's jammed car were there, Craig compensating for the wine performance by putting on a lordly air, dark hair falling dramatically to one side of his forehead, the petite blonde Cheryl nestling against him in a theatrically flowing dress. They seemed to have made up once more.

Cheryl came to the desk to see what I was doing.

'You're so lucky,' she said softly, 'working here in this wonderful place.'

'It's what I'd wanted to do all my life. And yet …' Yet, you get unexpected things, Sibanda had said. A gap had formed between my arrival at the reserve with my father and this moment here with Cheryl leaning almost wonderingly over the desk. I did not know how I could explain the gap to her; I was not even sure I could explain it to myself. It seemed easier to change the subject. I asked Craig, 'You never found the dinosaurs?'

He looked superior. 'Don't remember a bloody thing, if you're talking about the bridge.'

'Well, it was quite a good performance.'

The comment received a poor reception, but at least they were satisfied with their stay. As they left the office Cheryl paused in the doorway, gazing out across the wilds. 'I'm going to take all this back with me.' Her shapely arms stretched out wide. 'The vastness; everything living its own way as if humanity is simply irrelevant, didn't matter.' She seemed very secure in the idea, hands stroking her flow of light hair as she lowered them. 'That takes you beyond yourself, even beyond limited humanity.'

A confident shake of her head spread hair all across her shoulders. 'Just to have the feel of this vastness, this something-beyond – it'll make me so much freer on the stage. I know it.'

Duma was standing near the door as she made her exit. He nodded, impressed; his look was of inner understanding.

As the party left he turned to survey me in the fading light. 'You really are beginning to look like a lawyer's clerk,' he remarked. 'Time to go to the pans.'

So we came to his favourite hide on the reed-lined spit. There I watched herons as they flew in to roost. This was to be part of a special research project I had chosen: roosting behaviour. But late that afternoon at the water's edge, as I tried fixing my mind on the clambering, raucous mass of herons and white egrets …

How would that lot look after a hailstorm?

The question drifted into my mind like a cold fog, making me lower my field-glasses with a thwarted grunt.

'What's up?' Duma asked, turning from the water to look at the waterside trees now collecting a white bloom of egrets.

'Wonder what a hailstorm, like the one we had yesterday, would do to those egrets,' I said rather stupidly, perhaps simply because I couldn't make sense of them.

Duma surveyed the white-laden trees.

'Most birds would get killed of course. Why d'you ask?'

'I almost feel like saying, if God doesn't care about all those egrets, why should I? What do we make all those ordinances for, just for God to break?'

He looked impassively into the water lapping round us before murmuring, 'Rob, I'd say that's your problem, not mine. Why not just think of what Cheryl said?' A sweep of his hand took in the full length of the pan. 'All this can take you beyond yourself, she was saying. That implies that it can take you beyond your preconceived ideas of how the place should work.'

I raised my field-glasses thinking, who said I didn't know how this place works? and tried to fix my mind on the herons again. The sunset was fading to a little patch, yellow-orange, and was being picked up dingily in the pan. 'At least,' I thought vacantly as I stood there, 'I'm giving some mosquitoes a meal, if I'm not doing much else.' They were coming out in hundreds and I could hear Duma slapping at them.

'Wouldn't like to spend the night down here with your herons,' he muttered. '"Nature's social union" has a distinctly exploitative side to it.'

After a while he looked round to me. 'How's it going?'

'Too dark to see much, now.'

'Right.' He turned away from the pan and began making his way back to the Land Rover. 'Then let's get back to camp – that's if Chris has left any of it standing.'

That cold fog, the strange dark feeling that had drifted into my mind as I watched the egrets … a walk round the camp did not dispel it. The student group was quiet as the night sky, and a creeping inner uncertainty followed me to bed.

Chapter Seven

It was question time next day as Duma made sure I knew the ordinances. The student party trooped into the office to settle their accounts with Sibanda. Again the sparkling Cheryl came to my desk, eager to experience, to share in all that the reserve had to show her.

'What are you doing now?' she asked. 'Don't you ever get out among the animals?'

I hardly felt like telling her I was in effect sitting an exam. I merely quoted Chris: 'You can say that a ranger's job is more like desk-driving than bush-bashing. Requisitions, ordinances, log sheets, that sort of thing.'

She gave an encouraging, open-faced look. 'But it must be terribly important.'

Her positiveness, the clearness in her expression, took away any quick reply. I contemplated her face for a moment before quietly saying, 'And it's terribly important for someone like you to come here and say that kind of thing.'

Her look turned to one of understanding, of appreciation. She gave a little curtsy as if receiving applause before vanishing out of the office after the others.

Towards sundown, as Duma came into the office with Nsundu, 'What about my project on herons?' I asked. 'I'm getting that lawyer's clerk look again.'

Nsundu laughed. 'He's frightened of losing his suntan. Eah! What'll all the girls visiting camp think of that?'

Duma laughed too. 'All right, Rob, pack it in. Come, Nsundu, let's all go down to the pan.'

After a day in the office the fullness of evening in the bush came almost as a surprise. The openness, the clearness, the gentle breeze; 'This is the life,' I found myself thinking – perhaps thanks to the bubbly Cheryl – as the three of us drove down to the pans. Then, standing beside the big pan at the start of frog-call, 'This really is the life,' I said out loud, perhaps telling it more to myself than to anyone else. And Duma let out a great bellow, pointing to one end of the pan and then the other as the echoes came back. The space so defined was his space, our space, the bush's space; it was all one, we were all in it, and there was no need for talking.

Not at any rate on that evening. The next evening was different.

'When you tread a narrow path,' runs an African song, 'carry your child on your side, not on your back. You do not know what's behind you.'

I had a child, a concern, that might better have been left in its hut a few days. But the next evening at the pans I was holding it to me. And I was fearful of what might be behind me. The child was a cause of worry.

That evening was the close of my fifth day, the day of the foot patrol with Nsundu and Makanya along the northern boundary, the day of ending a cub's life and the raising of new questions where no question had been imagined before. A day of futility was setting, and now, trying to make something of the milling herons, there seemed to be an evening of it.

There was an added futility: carrying a child, grimly nursing the idea of some God-revealing purpose and meaning in nature, an idea I had carried all my life as the son of a missionary, an idea on that evening, after shooting the cub, I was clutching to my side – do not carry it on your back, you do not know what is behind.

Duma was the only other person at the pan that evening. His mood was distant; possibly it was all the arranging he had to do before leaving that left him sitting, staring vacantly into the water as I scanned the roosting-trees with field-glasses.

As the waterside trees again collected their bloom of white egrets I lifted my notebook to start making entries, wondering how the entry would look: Hail wiped out the roost this evening. God's contravention of Ordinance 1/1a.

Not the best entry for starting a heron project.

'Damn,' I muttered as I lowered my field-glasses.

'What's wrong?' Duma was still gazing into the water.

'Oh, nothing. I – I was just thinking about something that, that hadn't occurred to me before.'

'Well that's not too bad, Robert.' His reply had a touch of humour. 'I reckon that's something you should cultivate.'

'What d'you mean?'

'Mean? That old saying: the mills of the gods grind slowly, but grind small. Why not let them grind, Rob? Allow them what they need – such as things that hadn't occurred to you before. Your own, new, direct experience. Why not take it all on board like Cheryl seemed keen to do?'

Not this kind of experience. I repeated my question of yesterday evening: if God doesn't care about all those egrets, why should I? And Duma merely repeated his comment: that was my problem, not his.

But how could it be left like that? I turned on him. 'Not your problem? It's everyone's problem! Things like that cub shot today –' a feeling of urgency now – 'it's everyone's problem; must be. Don't you see? One *has* to make sense of it, somehow. If there's no plan, no design, then …'

'Then,' he said blandly, 'you could say there's no Planner or Designer either.'

'Then there's no meaning to life! Then it's – it's the total shambles Chris said it was; some kind of senseless, mindless machine.'

It was getting dark now. Duma stood up to give the reeds a last scan through his field-glasses before walking slowly across to the Land Rover.

'Rob.' His speech was as slow and deliberate as his pacing. 'Don't think I'm pretending this is cut-and-dried and that we really know very much. We don't. But for the moment, why not keep to perspectives we can actually see, and not mess around making up our own perspectives just because they look more comfortable?'

His powerful figure stopped for a moment in the gathering dusk.

'Look around you here. What do you see? Basically, it's a pretty good free-for-all, isn't it? Astronomical reproductive rates pitted against astronomical mortality. Things being born by the million, dying by the million. That's the hinge of fate for every species, every day. Even with the balance tipped right, there's colossal mortality; when the balance is not tipped right, then there's the slipway to extinction. And isn't that actually where most species end up, if the fossil record has anything to tell you? Massive extinction. Whole groups of animals and plants, dinosaurs and whatever – *gone.* All gone! Does that really give you much sign of an organized plan – or Planner – that any species, any individual, can rely on?'

Look around you; what do you see? A game of snakes and ladders? Mostly snakes, tailing down to extinction? And a couple of ladders – for the opportunists, beating along any direction that has the immediate pay-off of better survival and breeding.

He gave me a candid look. 'Can't you do better, Rob, than hang onto an idea of some string-pulling planner or designer, who step by step makes the whole thing go the way he wants it to go? Unless it's a designer who actually *likes* seeing mass slaughter, and species going extinct all the time.'

'Then all that's left is a slipway to personal extinction – to spiritual death, to disbelief. And then you cannot make *anything* of nature.'

Duma glanced at me thoughtfully. 'Maybe you'll think differently about that, Robert, in time.'

By the time I've gone bush-mad? When you tread narrow path, carry your child on your side; but where do you carry your child when the path fades out among thornbush?

That night, unable to sleep, I wrote a letter to my father. He was fond of Einstein's saying that God does not play dice with the cosmos. But is God not partial to snakes and ladders?

Chapter Eight

A letter came from my father almost by return of post.

The mail arrives about midmorning on most days, depending on the weather; in very wet weather it may be held up a day or more. I was in the office when it came, working with Sibanda on a charge, a poacher I had caught the day before. People living round the reserve can buy inexpensive meat gained from culling, but there are always those who chance an adventurous kill, ignoring any principles of resource management. One of them had become my first nick, and now I had to be sure I wouldn't spoil the case on a technicality.

Once more I was having to work through the ordinances.

'Letter for you, Robbie.'

Sibanda had left me for a moment to sort the mail. 'It's got the mission crest – must be from the old man.'

He brought it across to me before picking up the draft charge, looking down his nose at it.

'Tell you what, Robbie. I'll be the magistrate. Now you try and make a case …'

With my father's letter in front of me it was difficult to play Sibanda's game. What he had said on my very first day was already coming home to roost: 'There is something about the bush that opens and frightens the mind. You start asking questions so new they scare you.'

But I did not feel like telling him that.

At last, coming to the end of the draft charge, Sibanda said, 'Well, it looks okay to me, Robbie. Better go and try it on the chief. He's still doing that grazing survey outside the camp gates.'

I picked up the draft, and also my father's letter. Before heading out of camp to Duma I slipped into my hut to see what had been written.

It was not long; two pages of his careful handwriting.

'Many a time we find ourselves pulled up short,' he wrote, 'just when we thought we had life's reins firmly in our hands. Your ardent dedication to a ranger's life – how precarious you find it now; and yet, Robert, how wonderful are God's ways, that through your very precariousness you have been toppled into central, vital questions of our faith, questions that perhaps you never would have woken to in the secure life of the mission. Purpose or no purpose: is creation merely a futile nightmare? What more central question could there be than this? Yet, as now you feel so keenly, can one sensibly deny that suffering and devastation stalk continuously through nature? For that matter, can one deny that many churchmen have dismally naive ideas on that score, either unaware of nature's deep tragedy and brutality, or even if aware, not caring to think too much about it?'

His writing looked a little heavier. 'Cast me among the unthinking group, if you will. But can you really exclude yourself, Robert? Perhaps it is only now in your life that a situation has woken you to that painful task of really thinking – thinking, I mean, about fundamentals such as this.'

The writing seemed to pick up again with renewed confidence. 'Is nature really a futile nightmare? Robert, never forget that from the very beginning, God has bestowed on creation …'

Bestowed a game of snakes and ladders? Lots of huge, fat snakes and a couple of rickety ladders? I shook myself as if trying to throw something off … but was there a sneaking feeling that my father's ideas themselves could be poised to tumble down a snake, too? I gripped the page, creasing it slightly as I read on. 'Remember,' the letter was saying, 'remember that creation has a supreme gift – sometimes it might seem a terrible gift: the gift of freedom. It is a gift that makes creation the living, ever-new realization of divine Law, not the mere working of a mechanical toy, the lifeless adherence to some rigid "plan". Freedom, creation; they permit betterment. But – and here is the crucial point – with the gift of freedom comes the possibility of error, uncertainty, futility and suffering. It is so important to understand this, Robert, because if we do, then can we not see why we are in an imperfect world, a world filled with tendencies towards destruction as well as towards progress? And do we not …'

'It's missing the point,' I muttered as I put the letter down. What freedom was there for the animals slashed open by hail? Or those abandoned to hyaenas in infancy? The letter might work for people and their choices, but did it show any sign of tackling this side of nature, a side that I was now supposed to be doing something about, protecting creation against its own Creator? The question raised after the hailstorm still remained: in becoming a ranger, was I to defy this Creator, or merely judge him to be inept?

The question hung darkly over my father's letter as I shook myself into remembering I had to take Duma the case against the poacher. Why fuss about the case anyway? Isn't there a bigger case against God? I felt I couldn't be bothered about anything, didn't want to see anyone, or think about anything. Why think? It just brings a whole lot of trouble, going bush-mad like this. So just do what you're told to do and paid to do, and don't think … I looked blankly at the charge sheet for a few moments, picked it up mechanically and set out on foot to Duma.

All over the reserve were fenced-off squares where the vegetation was allowed to grow without being cropped or trampled by game. These squares became reference points for gauging how badly the bush was being punished by the animals living off it. Exclosures, the blocks were called; this one a hundred metre square of dense bush quite different from the browsed clumps of thickets outside the fence. I found Duma up a ladder propped against a hefty corner post, tightening the top wire.

'These rhino,' he called down as I came near. 'They think the corner poles are rubbing-posts put up specially for their benefit – they almost pushed this one over last night. And the more barbed wire you wind round the poles the more they seem to like it.'

'Did any game get inside?'

'Haven't looked yet. You climb in Rob, and see if you can find any spoor.'

'All right. Actually, I came to show you the charge against that poacher.'

'Oh, shove it in the Rover; I'll look at it later.'

I climbed over the fence into the exclosure and began checking for footprints just inside.

'I want you to keep a proper tab on these exclosures while I'm away,' he shouted to me. 'That's something I still have to show you: the maintenance and burning programmes for them.' As I came closer I heard him mutter, 'Hell, I'll be surprised if I can get everything finished before I leave. And I reckon by the time I leave, Rob, you'll have your head so full that you won't know whether you're coming or going.'

I felt his remark had more significance than he could have guessed, but I did not say anything. I carried on past him round the corner, looking for spoor almost as though trying to rub out everything in my mind by doing this simple and ultimately meaningless task.

'What are you gaping at?' I heard Duma shout. 'Has a leopard got in or something?'

I pulled myself together with a start; I must have been staring into the ground like an idiot.

'No,' I shouted back. 'No, it's all right.'

Hurriedly I did my round just inside the fence, coming back again to face Duma.

'Nothing seems to have got in – there's no spoor anywhere. Nothing's got in.'

Duma, still on the ladder propped against the corner post, paused to survey me for a moment.

'Any idea what's got into *you*, Rob?' he asked quietly.

There was a fumbling for words, while he looked at me with interest. He seemed completely untroubled – and that began almost to annoy me.

He stepped down to the ground outside the exclosure. 'Looks as if some of your own fencing has got knocked down,' he said.

'How d'you mean?' I asked through the fence.

'Think of fences inside us. Don't we erect fences to close off our habit-formed, habit-bound selves? Exclosures from the real, living world?'

He paused. An arm was raised against the post as he looked thoughtfully into the ground.

'You know, Rob, the way I see it ...' He turned to look out across the vast expanse of bush beyond the exclosure. 'The way I see it is this. The switch from the mission to the reserve: it's something that gives you the chance of breaking out of that exclosure of yours; something that might have got overgrown, stale, because new ideas, new ways of experiencing, have carefully been fenced off. Put it another way: here, now, you have the chance of cutting adrift from your habitual moorings, and being given the freedom to have a lot of fun exploring life and living. And yet ...' he turned thoughtfully to me, 'I imagine the way you see it is different. It's taken you by surprise, and now you're more like someone trying to tie himself madly back to the mooring post, shouting and pointing at all the crocodiles he might drift to if he's cut loose.'

'Well I can't say that I see where a "lot of fun" comes in.'

Very simply, he said, 'Most people don't.'

His sheer simplicity checked my thinking for a moment, but – no, there was certainly nothing simple about this. Had he any idea of what could be at stake … at stake – moored to a habitual stake? Coming adrift – that in a way matched what I felt. Either I could be in danger of drifting from the idea of a God-revealing nature, or it from me. Whichever way round, it seemed to be happening on an ocean of futility. And the drifting: perhaps there was the feeling of drifting toward something sinister, disastrous. Crocodiles!

Yet did he really know?

'Most people,' I said, 'don't find coming adrift from "habitual moorings" any fun at all. Especially if it's from the completeness given in a church life. Why should they?'

I received a very direct look. 'Because most people haven't the faintest damn idea what is really happening inside them. No idea what is drifting, what the drifting is away from, or even what the drifting actually is. If they had an idea, or even if they simply treated the thing as an open bit of exploration, then they'd handle their trip very differently. A reassessment of self and all that goes with it – that's about the most interesting thing that can ever happen to a person.'

A look of intense feeling etched into his face as he gazed out over the bush again. It seemed at first that he was not going to say any more. But after a few moments he turned back to me.

'Have you ever really thought of it, Rob? Real exploration, research into living. If your life is to have much value to yourself, to others, then, can you avoid it? And you have to set out … how can I put it? Set out on it barefoot. One needs to set out in humble touch with the ground of one's own experience, without any ready-made, comfortable protection. Not fare well but fare forward is how T.S. Eliot put it; that's the only kind of trip that will bear fruit in the lives of others, of yourself – the growth of insight which barefoot exploration, true experience can bring. A barefoot pilgrimage. So ...'

His gaze returned towards the heated bush. 'So, if you don't feel you're having "a lot of fun" here at the moment, at this time which has such potential for exploration, for knocking over old fences, for freedom, should you necessarily be worried about it? You might even find yourself in the company of some notable religious figures – very great figures.'

After a moment of looking at him, I clambered over the fence and stood next to him outside the exclosure.

A little heavily I said, 'Perhaps you're right.'

Chapter Nine

Checking exclosures went on almost till sunset. Scorching its way to the horizon, the sun remained bright and harsh, draining all colour from the bush and turning it a silvery grey. The country looked wan. One could feel it yearning for a freshening shower of rain, but the sky was clear.

After work, on a small hill behind the rest camp I watched this and wondered. What a complex thing the bush must be! To my father it seemed to reveal the workings of God. To Chris it disproved the existence of God. To Sibanda – well to him it didn't prove or disprove anything. It was simply there. But its openness, its hugeness, its fearfulness – that, he saw, could open and frighten the mind and make one ask questions. And unexpected things happen when you start asking questions.

And Duma? What was the bush to him? Or what was he to the bush? There seemed a kind of exchange, each imparting life to the other. For without people like the chief, this area would have been plundered by the most destructive creature on the planet. In return, the bush gave him something – some intensity of being – that I could not properly fathom, something I dimly felt during the talk in the exclosure. Its discovery, its realization, seemed one of the most important inner tasks now facing me. Even a religious task, he had said. A reassessment of self and all that goes with it, 'about the most interesting thing that can ever happen to a person.'

The start of a venture, of exploration – a pilgrimage of some kind, barefoot; that was the feeling the chief somehow had left with me. It seemed as risky as any exploration through the bush now spread out below me, with all its unknown dangers mingled with its splendour. Did the mind also have this vastness; in fact can you speak of mind? All you can sense is vastness. And so you fence off a bit and call it self; the bit you can live in, the bit that makes you feel safe – like this camp, fenced off from the wilds about it. Small wonder there is panic when the fence comes down.

Duma seemed to know this sense of vastness, achieving coherence without fences, something that in her own way Cheryl seemed to intuit. Perhaps as a drama student she had learnt the skill of putting self to one side, and she had come across inner foundations that gave security even in abandoning self. It was something that Duma recognised, nodding as he stood near the office door as she stretched out her arms to some vastness that they both sensed. But how do you come to know it? How do you reach into it, the kind of world the chief seemed to live in? Before I became a ranger it would barely have occurred to me that there was a question at all.

Then what about an answer?

The darkness now was closing in with the typical speed of the tropics. The sun had dropped straight down behind the horizon. After searing the bush all day, it appeared suddenly to have lost interest and gone off to do something else. Now the bush was stirring, and a new form of peril swept through it: a living peril, not one caused by heat and drought. The bush is a savage place in the darkness. The animals that seemed so timid during the day are now made fierce by the presence of death. Yes, there are the lions, booming the voice of fear and murder throughout the land. And the banal whoops of a hyaena, another who lives by death alone. Fear, there; not freedom.

What about an answer?

There below was the rest camp. It had taken over the sun's business of providing light – a Promethean intrusion into what was still left of mankind's own cradle. Could any child of this cradle have been more crudely delinquent than mankind itself? In a way I did not feel human at the moment; possibly this is something like the way God feels: detached, above. But God is supposed to love people. He is supposed to have given them his Son – and they promptly butchered him. If I were to walk down into the camp and tell them all to love one another, would they butcher me too? They would laugh at me. At least animals do not laugh at each other. No freedom there at the camp, either.

Then what about an answer?

Does God really watch these people? What would he watch? Wildebeest with their noses full of maggots?

The sun had left a red glow beyond the horizon, but this side of it I could see a little glow near the western guard post. No-one was supposed to be staying there that night, no fire should be there. I hurried down to alert Duma. On my way I met Sibanda. He had been called because a tourist party had not checked through the camp gates up to the time of closure.

'Robbie, what do you say? The tourist's car – has it caught fire out there? Won't be the first time that's happened.'

The chief had poachers in mind when I reported to him. He hurried up the hill with field-glasses and a two-way radio. It was almost dark now, but yes, he could see a small fire where the guard post was.

'Who the hell could be there?' he asked as I caught up with him. 'Shouldn't be anyone.'

Radioing the guard camps confirmed that.

'Could be those tourists, somehow stuck there,' I said. 'Lighted a fire for protection.'

'Could be any damned thing,' he said as we headed back to camp.

Nsundu was standing outside the office with Sibanda. In Zulu, 'I've been stuck in that office all day,' he said. 'I don't mind going out to see what's happened.'

I volunteered to go with him.

‘Then go well,’ Duma said. ‘It’s my turn to be stuck in the office, fixing things before I leave.’

We loaded some fire-fighting tackle into a patrol Rover and set out for the unknown.

As we headed for the western post our talk was mainly about bride payment. Nsundu was courting the daughter of a traditional family, and he had to prove his worth with a gift that befitted not only the bride-to-be but the whole family – a crippling burden for any young man.

‘It’s like male birds; they have to show off their feathers to prove they have good genes,’ he said contemptuously.

‘Well, let’s hope she’ll prove a better wife than that lioness, the one who abandoned her cubs.’

He shook his head. ‘That was not a good introduction to your life as a ranger.’

‘The chief didn’t seem to think it too bad. It made me think when I did not know how to think.’

‘And now, do you think you know how to think?’

‘Do you think you know how to think?’

‘We have small brains, just half a football, so we’ll never know how to think well.’

He was slowing down as, round a bend, a small car came into view.

It seemed, as we drew up, that it had been abandoned. Nsundu climbed out of the Rover with a torch and began to look for tracks.

The car was facing towards us, but behind it footprints showed that three people had headed away along the sandy road. It looked as if they were women’s prints. Nsundu examined the car more closely.

‘Look,’ he said, ‘the petrol cap is open. They’ve run out of fuel and the car starves to death.’

A funny way of putting it; I thought back to the starved lion cub: ‘Then you might as well shoot the car dead.’

He kicked a tyre. 'Dead already.'

We looked at the tracks again. I said, 'Maybe they noticed the guard post some way back, and they've gone there thinking they could get help.'

Nsundu snorted. 'And what made them think they could get there without being eaten?'

'I guess they were frightened out of their minds.'

Clambering back into the Rover, Nsundu began a slow drive following the trail of footprints. We started to notice irregularities, as if the people had been capering about.

'What do you make of that?' I asked.

'My brain is not big like a football to tell me.'

The road straightens out for two kilometres as it passes the guard post, to allow quick access. As we entered the straight we could see ahead a small fire at the post's turn-off. Nsundu's driving became even slower as we made out what was there in the fire light: three young white women completely naked, but starting to fling on some clothes as we approached.

By the time we reached them they had anxiously lined themselves up at the side of the road in front of the fire. One of them was holding a wine bottle. They were too lively to keep lined up for long; giggling and waving started as they saw two uniformed young men get out of the Rover. 'Dishy,' was one of the few coherent remarks I could hear.

I said to Nsundu, 'Do you have any cattle here that you can offer as bride payment?'

'Auu. I would not offer a bag of snakes for any of these.' According to Zulu thinking, what they were up to smelt of witchcraft. He left me to start negotiations.

It didn't take long. They had run out of fuel, although fairly well fuelled on wine. As the sun set they started to feel terrified as no other cars came by. Cell phones had been left at camp. One of them remembered seeing the guard post – a short distance away, she thought. So they set out, by this time fairly well tanked up with wine. Rollicking along, they thought that shouting and singing would keep any animals away. Yet by the time they reached the post and found no-one there they were becoming hysterical. So they pulled together some straw and rotted fencing poles, set them alight. 'Honestly, I don't know *what* got into us,' one of them said, 'but once we had a fire it all seemed so wild, so incredibly wild … we just took off our clothes and began dancing, dancing round the fire. I've never felt so, so, I don't know …' arms were flung wide, 'so *liberated*.'

'Back to nature,' another exclaimed. 'It was just all sheer magic.'

'You know what,' I said. 'For generations people have suffered terribly trying to discover Africa. Yet, I don't think any of them discovered Africa, its very heart, your heart, any better than you've just done.'

'You mean you aren't going to run us in?' asked the third, a little timidly.

'We're going to fuel up your car and run you home.'

When we reached their car the three Graces scrambled into it. One of them handed me the keys. 'You'd better drive – don't want to run into more trouble.'

As Nsundu emptied a can of petrol into their tank I said to him, 'You know, I can't begin to tell you what I've learnt tonight. About what I'm doing here in Africa, what for a flash I felt through those girls: total freedom, abandon. This is what the chief has been trying to get me to experience all the time. Freedom, liberation. Raw freedom.'

A gift of freedom that my father had never dreamt of.

Chapter Ten

Time in a game reserve far out in the bush is no keeper of regularity, no observer of civic measure, of weeks and weekends. Staff have one day off a week, but the days-off are staggered to allow continuity of maintenance, and often become forgotten as the weekly rhythm fades.

But the fourth day-off in my career as a ranger cannot be forgotten. It coincided with the morning of the chief's departure.

'You could do with a day's break,' he said, 'after this mad drilling you've had.'

Yet on that day, time on my hands became more wearing than hard work. I was at Duma's house before breakfast to see if I could help. But there were only his personal things to be packed and I would merely have got in his way. So I returned for breakfast and sat ruminating in my hut, not wanting to leave camp before he left.

To pass time I wrote to my father, but it turned out to be purely a news letter – the three Graces and their brand of freedom. I felt too unsettled in myself, too unsure of myself to touch anything deeper. When it was finished I took it to the office for posting. No-one was there, so I wandered slowly back to my hut, taking a long route past Duma's house.

'Hello, Robert,' I heard him shout from his study window. 'Like to come in for a while?'

'Can't I help in some way?'

'Thanks, but I've just got a few papers to sort now. Anyway, come in.'

He had made the spare bedroom into his study. There were brick-and-plank bookshelves against every bit of wall space except below the window, where he fitted his big wooden desk. As I entered I had to step between research papers strewn over the floor.

'Still haven't thought out what to take and what to leave behind,' he muttered, crouching on the floor as he sorted through them. 'Take a seat, Rob. Won't be long.'

An upright chair behind his desk was the only seat in the room. I settled there to pet one of his dogs. It seemed to be watching the packing uneasily. Duma glanced towards it for a moment with a slightly drawn face. 'Well at least I won't have to worry so much about my dogs, with you around.'

I grunted uncomfortably. 'It's a pity that the hunting dogs out in the reserve can't expect the same deal. I saw one with an injured leg yesterday, near the pans. Probably couldn't keep up with the rest of the pack, and there it was, alone, in pain, and starving. But what can you do about it?'

He surveyed me thoughtfully for a moment before asking, 'Still with problems, like it was at the pan one evening soon after you came here?'

I shrugged my shoulders. 'Well … sounds stupid, I suppose, but I'm not all that sure.'

'What do you want to be sure of, Rob?' he asked as he stood up.

I thought for a moment.

'I want to be sure of myself, for a start. Better being sure of one's self, than having the experience of your fences being knocked down. The open bush outside your fence frightens the mind, Sibanda once said.'

'Robert.' He pointed to his desk. 'See this wooden carving here?'

On his desk was a roughly carved, long wooden figure – it could have been a crocodile only it was more primeval, archetypal, than any particular kind of animal, with huge jaws, ragged teeth and a fierce, devouring look. The weirdness did not stop there; one side had been charred by fire.

'Well, quite honestly,' I said, 'I've wondered why you keep that thing in your study.'

He leant across the desk to lift it up.

'I'll tell you who made it.' He waved it in the direction of the north road. 'Someone I could take you to meet when I get back, if it interests you. A man who lives near the reserve, a man whom most so-called civilized people just pass off as a witch-doctor – just someone who makes a crooked living out of the gullibility of the folk in the bush around here. I prefer to call him an Elder.'

He rapped the carving against a pile of books on the table; they wobbled. 'I can tell you this. That man knows more about what goes on inside people than most of your fancy psychologists in the cities. One evening, sitting outside his hut round a fire, he showed me this carving and said, "This is the spirit that comes when I try to see what lies behind the world. It must eat me before that happens." I said, "D'you mean, self must be eaten before you get beyond self-blindness?" He nodded, "That can frighten you, it can scare you." I asked, "If it scares you, then where does this spirit come from: the water, your ancestors?" He laughed and almost shouted, "It comes from me, from me! And when I know that, then I'm no longer scared; I let it eat me and I can see!" And he threw the carving in the fire. I snatched it out, saying, "Let me keep this, so I can remember what you've just said." He replied, "Rather let it burn. I have to make many such carvings and throw them in the fire." But all the same, I kept it.'

He paused for a moment.

'Does that story say anything to you?' he asked.

I scratched my head. 'Connects with what Sibanda was saying about frightening the mind, I suppose. Maybe it connects with what you were saying at the exclosure – about cutting adrift from moorings, and getting into a panic about all the crocodiles one might drift to.'

'And what does that tell you about the crocodiles?'

'Get rid of them, of course. Otherwise you'll be dead.'

Thoughtfully he put the carving down on the table and gave me a steady look.

'Get rid of the crocodiles before you know what they are, and then you might really be dead,' he said bluntly.

'How d'you mean?'

'Supposing the self decides it wants to be sure of itself by becoming sealed off; sealed off from new experiences, from discovery, even sealed off from its self-made crocodiles that scare as they drag you out of your rut. Then all self is doing is making itself too dead even to become petrified. Isn't that what Cheryl was thinking about, when she said the wilds take you beyond yourself – see behind the world, as the Elder called it – and so make you free? Well then, aren't crocodiles a good thing if they help with that; clean up the old rotting carcass of self in a dead exclosure?'

I looked back at him indignantly. 'And d'you think I'm one of those who are fit for the crocodiles?'

'Rob.' His expression showed intense feeling, seriousness. 'Rob, don't think I'm getting at your father's religion; I'm not. But this is how it seems to me. It doesn't matter whether you think you're a Christian, a Hindu, a Muslim, anything else. As long as you sit wrapped up in self in an exclosure, blind, I reckon you're none of these, not in their deepest sense, anyway. Doesn't every great religion require a transcending of self, a dying to self, not just the wish to be sure of one's self?'

One part of me knew he was right – throw off your self-protecting clothes, dance free round a secret fire. But another part wasn't going to let me admit it. I pointed at the crocodile carving.

'Chris has told me that you quite often go to witch-doctors. But I didn't believe him – I'd never have thought you'd be interested in, in …'

He lifted the carving, thoughtfully, feeling its roughness. Then he eyed me severely. 'Depends what you – or Chris – mean by "witch-doctor".' The expression became more questioning. 'Tell me. After all your time at the mission, what d'you really know about these elders of the tribe?'

'Well, not very much, I suppose – not at first hand, anyway.'

'Then let me tell you this.' There was a new level of seriousness as he leaned over his desk towards me, holding the carving almost protectively in his powerful grip. 'If you care to take the trouble, you can learn a very great deal from some of these men; things that most so-called educated people don't know a damn thing about – in fact are even plain bloody scared to know about, sitting there in their tight little exclosures. And why?'

The tail end of the crocodile was dug into the pile of books, scattering them all over the table as his voice rose. 'Nearly all the people in our Western education, theology, science, universities, congresses – they deliberately close themselves to a lot of hard facts, experiences, things that in time will have to *revolutionize* our thinking.' Now he was almost on fire, waving the carving in the air. 'Yes! I've found it out here in the bush; in the East it's been common knowledge for centuries; and a few people are finding it out in the cities – right under the blasted noses of the intellectual Establishment. There are facts, hard facts. But what do most intellectual "top people" do? The facts don't fit their little picture of the world, so they scorn them, deride them, smear them, fence themselves off from them.'

I must have given him an astonished look. 'But – what sort of facts are you talking about?'

'Have you ever heard about someone being able to sit down, close his eyes – let in the crocodiles to get rid of self-blindness – and tell you what's going on any distance away? Like the man who made this carving can do?'

'That seems inconceivable.'

'Well then ...'

Suddenly he subsided, turning half round to sit on the edge of the desk.

'If it's inconceivable to you,' he said quietly, 'then it's no good my telling you about it, is it?'

'But wait a minute!' Now I was the one to get roused. 'How does this tie up with what you ... well, I mean, you're a pretty tough-headed biologist ...'

'Why does it have to tie up? Why should we think we know enough to tie all the facts together into neat, dead parcels?'

'I thought the aim of science was to tie things up.'

'That's fair enough as an aim. But let's try to get all the facts first, not throw away stuff that won't fit into the dead little parcels already tied up in the ivory towers. Rob ...' feeling was building up again, 'Rob, what I've said about you fencing things off; it's peanuts compared to how that ivory tower lot perform. And they'll thrash you if you start tugging at their fences; but with a little trouble you can discover things that blow most people's intellectual fencing to *shreds*. All you do is stop on the established road, and walk a few paces off it. Like really getting to know a Zulu elder. Then you'll see what a crappy little track that established road is – you actually *see* it. But if I shout back to people stuck on their track and say, "Hey, wake up, look around you, *experience*," all they do is think me a nit. "Too much of the bush," they say, even put up *more* fences on either side of their track. But a waking must come. You can't stifle facts forever. Then watch the crocodiles!'

Heavily he leaned over the table to collect the books scattered by the crocodile, muttering, 'Those clever people who just say a witch-doctor's thinking is primitive; who is really being primitive? Who's shutting themselves off from raw experience, yet having the bloody cheek to call it "science" – science that's supposed to be based impartially on experience, yet so screwed up it can't handle this wealth of human experience. Is that a good way of starting a new century?'

With a dismissive grunt he returned to his papers on the floor to scoop them up and drop them into a backpack. 'And here I am about to go into that tight, knotted little mess again.'

For a moment he gazed at the backpack, vacantly solemn, then rose, straightened himself as he looked at his watch.

'Rob, could I trouble you? Would you go and call Sibanda? I'm just about ready to leave now.'

'Okay. That's no trouble.'

No trouble at all – a walk between the camp huts, bright in the sun, helped clear my thinking. It was like this every time I got into conversation with the chief, a mental pounding; only this time it seemed more radical than ever, as if loads of ideas had been heaped on me to sort through while he was gone. Most of the camp had to be covered before I found Sibanda, and by the time we returned, Duma was already beside his packed Land Rover in front of the house, petting his dogs.

For the moment with his dogs he looked grim. Then a few last words with Sibanda and he opened the door of the cab.

'Goodbye, Rob.' He gave me a powerful handshake before climbing in. 'Let's look forward to what we'll find at our next meeting. Perhaps we both shall have changed – quite a lot. What do you think?'

I found myself wondering what I *could* think. Something given at this time of parting called for radical searching. I wondered dimly if Duma had actually planned it that way, open-ended, challenging, as, 'Goodbye,' was all I could say, 'and I hope you … that you have a successful time.'

'Bloody better be, if I'm going to be away from here for nine whole months.'

He started the engine with a roar and shouted back in Sibanda's language, 'Stay well, Lizard; stay well, Fawn!'

'Go well, Chief!' we cried, and waved back to him through the cloud of dust.

Chapter Eleven

That evening Sibanda asked Chris and me to his house for a beer. The house he lived in was built to the same plan as Duma's, between the rangers' huts and the office; but while Duma's house was filled with books, Sibanda's house was filled with people – these were *his* books, he said, from which you could read about life directly. The 'mobile spending library', Chris called his lively place. When we got there we found the door being opened for us by Martha, Sibanda's wife; Sibanda had just gone to lock the office, she told us. Short, rounded, nearly always with a beam playing in the valleys of her well-filled face, there came her usual 'How's our teacher?'; she had been a pupil at my father's mission school, and now to have his son here at the reserve was to her a kind of blessing. No blessing for me, though. In the upheaval of the past few weeks I'd been finding it more and more difficult to feel at ease with her.

She showed us to the sitting-room – a place she had managed to make look warm despite the regulation Game Department furniture, and in a moment Sibanda had joined us, handing out beer once his five children had been herded off by a grandmother.

'Must celebrate the chief's departure,' he said.

Chris raised his can. 'Here's to an outbreak of anthrax. That's a dead cert. as soon as he's gone!'

'You wouldn't look so smart if that actually happened,' Sibanda said, laughing. 'Pretty girl came into camp today. How about it, eh, Robbie?'

I swilled the beer round in my can without saying anything.

'How old?' Chris asked.

'You!' Sibanda laughed again. 'When you first came here you told me you were finished with women for life.'

'Aw, yes; but that was over two months ago. Parents wealthy?'

'Actually there's no joke. The father was in a car smash and hurt his brain. His wife says, it's changed everything – everything that he was before. Seems to have – what did she say? – wiped out his old personality, the brain damage. She just hopes a rest here will help him.'

Martha sighed. 'Eah! She has a heavy time with him. I helped her get him to their hut. He always wants to make trouble – but why is it like that, Robert? Why must the whole person change because the brain, the body, is hurt? The personality isn't a ... a thing like a body.'

'The personality,' declared Chris, obviously pleased with the sound of his remark, 'is nothing but an epiphenomenon of the physical brain. It's just a by-product of nervous functioning, that's all.'

'You don't say!' exclaimed Sibanda in mock wonderment.

'It's a fact! Hell, don't you know about the effects of brain surgery and chemotherapy on personality? If you alter the brain physically or chemically, then you change the personality; it's totally dependent on the brain. Here –' he held up his can – 'see what a beer can do!'

Sibanda also raised his can a bit uncertainly, and put down quite a big dose without saying anything.

'Of course,' Chris added, 'how can people say that the personality survives after the brain packs up at death? Impossible, but religious people ...' A hand passed emptily through the air to show it was too stupid even to talk about.

I said nothing. You just be careful, Robbie – Sibanda's warning on my first day came back to me. Don't go fighting with Chris. I turned to watch a cluster of little hairy caterpillars on the table leg. A moth had laid its eggs there, and now a so-called miracle of nature had occurred: the eggs had hatched. They would all die on the barren table leg, of course. God and Nature had not been provident enough to tell the moth not to lay its eggs there in the first place.

Martha had been watching me as if she expected some comment. When nothing happened she turned to Chris and said bluntly, 'We do survive death.'

His eyebrows rose questioningly. 'But how's it possible? You've just seen what happens with that man who came in: the personality is a product of the brain. So how can it go on when the brain finally packs up?'

Sibanda rubbed his head as if trying to think of some way to change the subject, but Martha, with a direct look at Chris, had already launched into a reply. 'You can't just say that something as real as a personality can go to nothing at death. You tell him, Robert.'

'A candle flame is real, isn't it?' asked Chris. 'But when the chemical reactions producing the flame stop, then the flame –' his hands opened emptily – 'is gone. When the chemical reactions that produce the personality stop, then the same thing happens.'

Martha looked at me again. It was easy to see what she was thinking: is this not the son of our teacher? Why, why is he not answering?

'Life would be nothing if we did not survive,' she said deliberately as if to give me some kind of cue.

Chris exploded. 'If we don't survive, then hell, we don't. You've got to alter the meaning you place on life; you can't alter the facts of life. And you can't get round the facts. How can you exist without a brain?'

She gave Chris a reproving glance. 'I suppose it's no good telling you that the Bible says we survive death.'

'Definitely no good!' He was leaning back in his chair, speaking expansively. 'The Bible as usual contradicts itself – the Old Testament doesn't support the idea. Anyway, it doesn't matter what those old scriptures – Bible, Koran – say. They're pre-scientific. What *can* you make of all the stuff they give out, like a heavenly father going round feeding the birds of the air, and adorning the lilies of the field? Huh! What do the lilies look like after they've been flattened by a herd of buffalo? And what do the chicks look like when they've been kicked out of the nest by a young cuckoo and starve?'

A sweep of the hand signified: you can believe nothing of that. 'And if you can't believe that, then where do you start believing? If the Bible knows nothing about biological realities, what good is it at knowing about anything else?'

Martha surveyed him coldly before asking, 'Where did you learn this poison? It comes out as freely as a cow passes water.'

He smiled grandly. 'It's nothing you learn. It's how you can think. And luckily I had a professor who really got me to think. What's poisonous about that?'

She turned her look from Chris to me, assessing clearly in her mind how poisonous it was.

'Incidentally,' Chris said to me, 'the prof said he might be coming here in a couple of months' time. Wants to do some research – parasite life cycles.'

'That's right,' Sibanda said a little reservedly. 'That prof of yours has booked in already. But it's a pity the chief won't be here. Strikes me the chief could pick a good fight with you and your professor on all this. The chief has lots of ideas on the subject.'

'The chief has some totally cuckoo ideas, if that's what you mean,' Chris retorted. 'Those witch-doctors and things: he has the whole of modern science against him – every single fact points the other way.'

Sibanda looked thoughtful. 'It seems that facts belong to different tribes, like tribes in people. And as with people, they don't always get on well together.'

He pointed to Chris, then to me.

'There is your tribe of facts, Chris; and then there is the tribe of Robbie's father: Western Christianity. Then there is my tribe: African Christianity – what you whites mix up with ancestor worship because we keep our African belief about the value and influence of family spirits – yes, real people living after their death, people we must honour. Then there's the chief's tribe – no, maybe the chief has no tribe. He is not a tribalist with facts, I think. But I tell you this, Chris: your tribe has a terrible poison if it can prove that all other tribes have empty people – that there really is nothing beyond our life on earth. Robbie, it makes nonsense of your father's religion, doesn't it? And it makes nonsense of mine too.'

'If there's nothing beyond physical life,' I said mechanically, 'nothing beyond this physical existence at all, then the basis of Christianity is just a farce.'

Nothing but futility.

'Then why not come clean with it?' Chris demanded. 'There aren't really different tribes of facts. It's just that people call any old belief a fact when it suits them. But these aren't facts at all. And the sooner we stick to science and get rid of all that tribal stuff the better, because *that,* that's the source of troubles worldwide, people being destroyed because of religious beliefs, not the real, actual facts themselves.'

'I still say there are tribes of facts,' said Sibanda. 'I think the chief is dealing with facts. And a lot of his facts are not your facts. And I don't think they are Robbie's facts, either.'

Chris suddenly looked bored. 'Well if you want to call stuff that isn't a fact a fact, then there's nothing I can do about it. Cheers!' He waved his empty can in the air.

Sibanda sprang across the room for more beer, relieved to have a change of subject. 'We'll go bush-mad if we carry on like this,' he said. A couple of cans were held up. 'You, Robbie? More?'

I shook my head dispiritedly, avoiding Martha's gaze at me.

'Looks like you need lots more,' Sibanda said.

'Looks like he needs a shot of strong coffee,' remarked Chris. 'What's bugging you now?'

Fences. This morning, with the chief, there had been a sense of challenge in having no fences, maybe even a touch of the freedom shown by the three wild Graces. Perhaps the chief was right in saying I was not impressive as a Christian. Yet then, this morning, that lead to exploration, research into living as he called it, not to futility. But now, what was there left in Christianity, in life itself to be impressed with? It had been like this every time Chris got going. Four weeks, and he had reduced me to wondering whether there was anything left in my religion that could not be flattened by the simple facts around me. A few remarks from him and it had shrunk to nothing; no mind, only fleeting brain function, fences and death.

'You have a terrible poison,' Sibanda had just said to him. I glanced at Martha. Behind the timeless African expression I could tell little of what she thought. But as she sat looking in front of her into the ground, she was no longer in the spirit of the party.

'I ... I've got a headache,' I said. 'Probably had too much sun today. I think I'll turn in.'

'You don't even want coffee?' asked Sibanda. He seemed a little put out. Martha said nothing, but now I could see disappointment, perhaps even bewilderment, in her look.

'Thanks, but some aspirin would be better.'

Out in the night air I stood beside my hut, watching some tourists leaning against the camp fence. Were they hoping to hear a lion, or maybe even the rasping cough of a leopard? But what could they really sense through the fences of conventionality? I pictured a rhino suddenly lunging at them out of the darkness, pulling the fence in streamers behind it. Yet that sort of terror would be mere diversion; the physical danger could bring almost welcome relief from an inner world with the fences in tatters, the familiar beacons toppling. I was ready for any physical dangers when I joined the reserve, but these dark tendrils of nothingness spreading, levering open, eroding – no, I had not been prepared for that. Even the lightness of Cheryl, of the three Graces, was fading after this blighted evening.

When I went to bed that night I did not pray. Pray to what? The answer facing me was only a bare wall beside my bed, a blank expanse of nothingness. Where do you start believing? Chris had asked. Easier to say where you stop believing. For if even the idea of survival, the very idea of some destiny beyond physical life could be made to look so much nonsense, then – your faith is vain.

'Most people don't know what problems are until they start working here,' Chris had said on our first outing. But cocksure and without much to lose in any case, had he any idea how far and how deep the problems stretch when you have to carry a child? – on your side, not your back; you do not know what's behind you.

Yet there seemed no way of getting round Chris's arguments, his point of view. The morning scene at the pans on my very first outing with the chief would not go away. I was saying to him that Chris's views were alienating; that they struck me as mechanistic madness. 'If I ever come round to believing what Chris thinks, then something inside me would have to die,' I was saying.

You have a terrible poison, Sibanda had said to him, but what antidote is there for his acid attack on our views? 'If you two start fighting,' Sibanda had warned almost the minute I got here, 'I don't want to have to go round picking up the pieces that you and Chris leave everywhere.' They were just words, then. I would never have believed that 'picking up the pieces' could apply to me.

Yet there seemed nothing, now, but fragments of a house once warm and solid that I believed was founded upon a rock. Now all I had were these scattered pieces, a heap of rubble exposed to a cold and mindless universe.

PART TWO

Chapter Twelve

In the African bush there is only today; yesterday has been eaten by termites and all we have left is what has survived the night. There is no history, only timelessness and the splendour, the terror, of now.

So three months as a ranger is not the record of a string of days spent working and a few taken off. Three months is an aspect of now, a colouring of the present. And the place, the aspect of space that frames this now, is Duma's study. Here and now intersect in the crocodile carving on his desk.

This carving: it almost vanished, not through termites, but through another of Africa's great destroyers, fire. The carving has to do with a self that fears its own fabric being destroyed. 'I want to be sure of myself,' I was saying two months ago here in the chief's study the day he left. His response was to show me this carving, the savage face of fear. He said, the more you try to be sure of yourself – the more you try to put up fences – the greater is the fear. Yet how do you break the cycle of fear making fences, fences bringing fear? What has to be done to get in touch with the chief's way of fearlessness, achieving coherence without fences, a state of clearness, of release ...

'Wakey, wakey!'

Chris was looking through the study window, head cupped dopily in his hands.

'Hey!' he shouted as I turned towards him. 'For Christ's sake, what are you doing in there? The head warden's just come!'

He drew himself up stiffly in mock official attitude. The warden acted as if the Game Department were a military organization, and his officious, rather mechanical air gave Chris all he wanted for his swipes at authority.

'McBraid, report immediately for an emergency briefing. Come on, jump to it there.'

'What's the trouble?'

'Dunno, but it looks like plenty. Nsundu's in the office with the general already. He wants all of us there, now.'

I put the carving back on Duma's desk and followed Chris.

'Come in. Good afternoon, McBraid.'

A Zulu, but I never heard the warden speak in Zulu. Short, portly, he had a face that was not easy to read. At the moment he was sitting, self-important, behind the desk going over a map Nsundu had spread out before him.

'What can you tell me, McBraid, about numbers and movements of lion in the northern sector?'

'Normally there's a loose-knit pride of seven in that sector, sir.'

'That fits what Nsundu says. And no old animals? Or young males being driven out of the pride?'

'No, sir, not in that sector.'

He stared at me blankly as though he had a problem that was all my fault. 'That does not make it easier.' He tapped the map with a stubby finger. 'The police, they say at least one lion in the northern sector has taken to marauding outside the reserve. Man-eating. Happened early this morning.'

He leant back in his chair and twirled a pen.

'And now I want information, details. Duma said before leaving that the northern area is overstocked with lion, but he never gave me a report. You rangers will now have to report. Lion distribution, availability of prey, physical condition of the marauder, other things like weather, water, fencing. Any lions that go always outside the reserve must be destroyed; our aim is to control the remainder.'

He was now standing up and packing his brief-case.

'Pickerell and McBraid, you must to go to Mkomo village and report at the police post, find out what is happening. Take firearms with you, but you must work with the police.' He looked at his watch. 'If you leave now you can reach Mkomo before dark. I shall go with Nsundu through the main north gate to check the game guards there. I shall spend the night at Sengwe, near the north gate. You must realize this situation is very serious and –' he eyed Chris – 'you must show responsibility all times.'

With that we were dismissed.

'Well,' Chris said as we walked to our huts, 'at least he's enjoying it even if no-one else is. He's performing like it's a bloody campaign.'

'Eah!' said Nsundu. 'And this kind of weather to choose for it.'

It was a dull, heavy day. Rain had been falling for nearly a week, the first set-in rains of the season, and the whole reserve had a feeling of relaxation, almost lethargy. The frantic struggle for existence seemed eased; the game was not lying up in dense bush, but had dispersed and could be seen standing about in the open with the casualness of domestic cattle. The softening rain had brought a feeling of passiveness; it was not a time for moving about and being strenuous, even though it was cool. Certainly not a time for trying to get somewhere in a hurry by road – that was obvious from the moment Chris slithered the patrol Rover out of camp, only just missing a gate post. Once he had spun onto the north road he became less chatty as he struggled between keeping the vehicle steady on the road and keeping it moving at all.

Silence suited my mood; I gazed vacantly ahead, sometimes at the sodden road, sometimes at the sheet of muddy water that covered the windscreen after Chris had dashed through a puddle. It was all the same, amounting to nothing.

As we came to a firmer piece of road, 'I'm bloody sure our lions aren't causing any trouble up there,' Chris muttered. 'There could be a whole pack of lions living outside the reserve without the police knowing the first thing about them. It's probably a couple of ritual murders, anyway. What'd our lions be doing at Mkomo?'

'I suppose they followed the game into the sandveld when the rains broke, and then carried on after cattle. The sandveld is bad hunting country for lion, and cattle do get into the reserve up there – cattle-herders keep cutting the fences.'

There was silence until we reached a turn-off, where Chris slowed down.

'Are you thinking of taking the short cut to Mkomo?' I asked.

'Why not?'

'Shouldn't we keep to the main road in this weather?'

'It'll be better on the sandy track than in all this mud.'

We lurched to one side as he swung off the main road. 'And it's much quicker – if we get there at all.'

I lapsed into silence again. Who cared if we didn't get there? Chris was still having a hard time, but he enjoyed what

Duma called his rodeo stunts. We said nothing until we were close to the northern boundary.

'Hey!' Chris exclaimed slowing down. 'See that?'

'What?'

'Pugmarks, there on the track. We're with the boys!'

He stopped, and we climbed out to look. Sure enough the spoor of a lion was plainly marked in the moist sand.

'And it's going our way,' he said.

I looked at the imprints more carefully. 'It seems that a couple of toes are off one paw. Makanya has spoken about this one – got caught in a snare.'

'Damaged paw, eh?' Chris had the air of an expert. 'Predisposing factor for man-eating.'

As we climbed back into the Land Rover I hoped we would be able to start again. With a man-eater around, this was not the place to get stuck.

'That paw'll give us a good lead,' Chris said as he let out the clutch. The wheels gripped and we moved on.

Now he shifted his attention from the lion spoor to the dark, low-lying cloud masses that were rapidly collecting.

'It'll be the last bloody straw if we get hauled out on a patrol in the middle of a downpour tonight,' he said. 'We'll have to shoot them a line about lions staying at home on nights like this. Look! Where's he gone now?'

He pointed to the track. The pugmarks had disappeared.

'We're coming to a temporary watercourse,' he said. 'Maybe he's heading up that.'

'I wonder what the drift across it will be like. I still reckon you shouldn't've come this way.'

'That's what you think! The sand there'll be hard – better than this stuff.'

The sight of the lion spoor was now working on him. 'I was just thinking of that scene at Kima. A man-eater opened the door of a railway carriage where three hunters were sleeping, and made off with one of them through a window, leaving the other two rigid with bloody fright. How'd you've like to've been in there?'

I grunted.

'It's amazing how determined man-eaters get,' he went on expansively. 'They'll break into anything. Hell, I dunno how many reports there must be of lions clawing their way into huts – even jumping on top of outbuildings and tearing away the roofing. Imagine being locked in a room with a man-eater pulling up the roof above you!'

'It'd drive you out of your mind.'

'Well it's happened more than once. Sleeping people have even been dragged out of their cars. So, what stunt is *our* little specimen going pull off?'

He became silent again as attention switched to the tricky driving. The track curves down a slight bank before meeting the watercourse, a sandy trough that carries water after a heavy storm. Normally he would whirl round the curve, throwing up a wake of sand, but now he took it more cautiously until he saw there was no running water. Then he accelerated, gathering speed to help ride – so he thought – over the silty sand.

Soon he was in trouble.

'Hell! The bloody sand's softer than I thought.' He slammed into low-range gear. 'As long as we keep moving we'll be all right.'

The vehicle began to judder; it seemed to be making no progress at all. Then it crawled on again like a stricken beetle, staggered, and began embedding itself in the soft silt.

'God!' he groaned. 'We'll have to put some branches under the wheels.'

We climbed out to see. He was right; the wheels had half disappeared in sand.

Chris was starting to look frightened. 'Hope that fucking lion isn't around here.'

'Well, let's start chopping,' I said tersely.

We each took a machete and made for the side of the watercourse, hacking down branches to pack under the wheels, then more branches for laying in front of the Rover to carry it over the rest of the drift.

'Okay,' Chris said when we had laid the track. 'Let's try to get this bloody thing moving. You check the wheels.'

He climbed back into the cab and started the engine. Cautiously he let out the clutch.

'Stop!' I shouted. 'It's just digging itself in.'

'Right up to the bloody axles,' he said as he climbed out to look underneath. 'The sand's got no cohesion and we're not fitted with a winch to haul ourselves out.' He grabbed the only spade and began to dig frantically. 'We'll just have to pack more branches under the wheels.'

I started clearing another wheel with my hands, but almost jumped as a tremendous crack of thunder split the heavy stillness.

'That's just what we need now,' moaned Chris. 'A big bloody storm.'

'We're going to get it, too,' I said, looking up at the swirling grey clouds. Big drops of rain were already beginning to fall.

Chris let out a sour 'Bugger!' as he stabbed the spade into the silt. 'Well there's no point in getting wet. Better wait in the cab; when it lets go like this it usually clears soon after.'

We climbed back into the Rover as rain started to lash the vehicle to great booms of thunder.

Chris was looking exhausted after the heavy driving and his scramble to free the Rover, but it didn't take him long to feel bored, and he began fidgeting.

'All we need now is for the bloody stream to come down in flood. How long's this goddam storm going to last?'

'It's still coming down in buckets.'

He opened his door and leant down to look at the wheels.

'Huh! We can forget about driving this contraption to Mkomo tonight. The silt's being washed right around the wheels. It'll take a caterpillar tractor to haul us out.'

Almost drenched, he pulled himself back into the cab and began mopping his head with a handkerchief. Then, 'Flaming, sodden hell,' came through a frustrated sigh as he curled back in his seat and put his left foot irritably against the dashboard.

Rain drumming on the cab roof and a grey blankness all round us – certainly there was nothing more we could do. Before long Chris was beginning to nod. A bit more fidgeting, an impatient glance at the greyness outside now turning to darkness, and finally he curled back further in his seat with a grunting 'Well, I've done *my* day's work.'

Soon he was fast asleep.

In the darkness the rain stopped almost as suddenly as it started. Chris was still sleeping heavily and I climbed out of the cab with a torch to see what had happened to the wheels. It was as bad as Chris said. They had half disappeared in silt. In the dark, walking the rest of the way to Mkomo seemed uninviting with a man-eater somewhere about. But no-one would start looking for us till next morning when the warden and Nsundu arrived at Mkomo and found us missing.

I muttered a 'Damn!' to myself as I clambered back inside the cab, fuming at Chris for being careless enough to get us stuck here at all.

His talk about lions being able to smash windows, drag sleeping people through car doors – that was no exaggeration. When I read stories about man-eaters at the mission, I would be left with a churning imagination and felt on guard for the rest of the evening. What was happening now had the ingredients of a nightmare, sitting here engulfed in darkness in the middle of a man-eater scare and with fresh spoor only a few hundred metres down the track. The lion was possibly lurking in this very watercourse …

The storm had left the bush silent, with a feeling of oppression. Silence in the African bush is not a sign of peacefulness, inactivity, safety. It is a cloak for the most fearful things in nature. Even an elephant could approach from behind and prepare to beat you into the ground, yet nothing would be heard. In the silence the dark, ancient powers of the bush become inner realities; there is an atmosphere of charged tension, of prowling, swiftly-darting terror, of lurking, supple death. The hunters of the bush cleave through the night as though caught by some primeval force, and with supreme control slink, hover, strike without a sound. The living wilderness is seized and held by powers as old as fear itself, and fierceness ripples through the bush, tensing hunter and hunted alike. Each shrub becomes an ambush, the waving grass a mask; nowhere can safety be found, there is no refuge. Not one individual can escape the struggle for existence, no species can avoid the judgement that fitness endlessly imposes. The wilds become hushed with the presence of death.

Neither accepted nor rejected, the void of death passed through me in the silence, chilling, evacuating the few remaining pieces left over from that house once founded – so I thought – upon a rock. The void could no longer be kept out. It fell amongst the ruins of a settled world, a world three months away yet displaced now by a life. Not even a heap of rubble seemed left as I stared vacantly through the window at the night sky, beginning to show in patches through the clouds. Up there were bits of Orion, Aries, the Pleiades – but could these be the stars that shone upon my father's mission, stars I had absorbed in wonder such a little time ago, such a little distance away?

These here were different stars, coldly distant, stars that were as mindless as the bush splayed out beneath them.

And in the void, slowly I clambered out of the Land Rover to be under those stars, to stand in this emptiness. It was some final gesture, in which emptiness could enter emptiness, a vacancy where even deadly things are part of nothingness, crocodiles within and lions without, all becoming empty as not even a within or a without is finally left intact. And as I stood emptily in this emptiness, it was enormously still. No within, no without; somehow it was gigantically still.

Strange, to be so gigantic when quite so empty. Yet perhaps if there is no within, no without, no portioned-off self – although awareness is still there – then in this opening out what else could there be but unqualified vastness? A wonder felt by the intuitive Cheryl?

This nothingness beneath the stars: it had the feel of some huge no-thingness, full of thingless potentiality, boundless, timeless, empty of separate things yet somehow making things appear and happen. Could it even be this, this puzzling vastness-behind-things, that the elder came upon when he tried to find 'what lies behind the world'? When he let crocodiles do their work on self?

Could this be it?

Then how do you reach into it, this giant emptiness?

By being empty, too? Also being empty? Throw self-made crocodiles in the fire, throw self in the fire? Perhaps yes; perhaps you start by stealing beyond those bushes now made a closing wall by the darkness. Pass through them, pass into them, a new participation as, gliding through the forms around you, you enter some kind of formlessness which creates those forms – what lies behind the world, primordial. Yes, a new kind of seeing as self and its fear crumble. Gently in a flush of strange excitement I slipped out towards the bush as though passing through a veil separating thingness from some immense behind-thingness; then up the watercourse … and into a void of time.

Is this what fired Duma? For the first time, even after all my years in the bush, was I only now seeing into its hidden livingness, even for the first time seeing into myself, being also a part of this livingness, part of this vastness as inner becomes outer and outer inner; not a self-subsistent thing at all? This was a new existence. In a moment of dissolution, surrender of self, in the terror of life and death, a secret door had slipped open to reveal – what? – nameless vibrancy, luminosity, creativity, unity, a wealth only to be unlocked by total emptiness …

And then I heard a grunt to one side.

A lightning bolt shot through me, a living electrocution; I could hear almost nothing through the pounding of blood, but – now the sound again. Woop, woop. I started, listened more … and collapsed laughing. A huge bullfrog had discovered a patch of water. It was inviting anyone interested to bed down in it.

I wooped with the serenader till it became frightened and stopped. Then I pranced back to the Land Rover to tell Chris what had happened.

He was still asleep, so I climbed on top of the cab roof and from this height surveyed the bush, dissolving myself in it. Flushed with life, I could scarcely make out what had happened. In a moment of emptying self it seemed that a whole maze of other distinctions had been emptied. Fences had evaporated; exclosures, enclosures, a crazy network of life-limiting barriers had gone, and somehow I was no longer a closed-off centre, anxious, self-concerned. There seemed more to me, to other things, to our whole interaction and union, more to this participation and vastness than could ever be contained in one life, my life. No longer could there be an isolated existence; whatever existed now was an awareness with no clear bounds, liberated, cleansed and strong, wanting to go hurtling off into the bush again.

I wished Duma could be here to stride out with me. This is how the chief must feel – intense, free, living abundantly, something like the magical dance of the three Graces. I was about to jump down and wake Chris when the cab light went on below.

'Hey, Rob!' he called sleepily.

I heard him open his window. 'Robert!' he shouted. There was a touch of alarm in his still sleepy voice.

More silence.

Chris opened his door and began to climb out. As he was about half-way I leant over and gave a low growl above him.

In a flash he sprang back into the cab, slamming the door and feverishly closing the window until he registered laughter from above the cab.

'You bastard!' he shouted, leaping out but still quite shaken. 'You're bloody lucky I didn't put some shots through the roof!'

I jumped down still speechless with laughter while Chris walked irritably round the Land Rover checking the wheels with a torch.

'Well,' he said sourly, 'when you've finished wetting yourself, let's try to get this bloody thing moving. The sand's compacted and should be easier to handle.'

He grabbed the spade and dug furiously.

'You'd better mount guard in case there actually *is* a man-eater around,' he added huffily.

Within half an hour we were on our way again.

Chapter Thirteen

By nine o'clock we reached the trading store, the trader's house and a police post strung along a sandy road, all that Mkomo village amounts to apart from a few huts clustered nearby in the bush. As we approached, the only sign of life came from the lighted police post.

'We'd better go and present our credentials,' said Chris driving up to the box-like little building.

The constable on duty seemed rather surprised that so many people should appear on the scene of what was to him fairly commonplace. Makanya had already headed some game guards through the area. Where his tribe lived, the constable said, man-eating attacks were a routine happening in the wet weather.

'I suppose,' he said in Zulu, 'that here you are worried because the lions belong to you. You game people value lions in the same way that other people value cattle. It is simply *business,* not so?'

He leant to one side, face split by an enormous grin.

Then a serious look: a woman had been ambushed and killed early in the morning on a path leading to a watering-place. Also there had been reports of stock losses.

'Our station commander - hau, he is a great hunter!' The constable was beaming again. 'He knows everything about lions, especially about where they will not be, because that is where he always sets his traps and bait.'

'Is he out hunting tonight?' I asked.

'No. He said he had something to see to at Sengwe.'

'I know what that something is,' Chris muttered. 'A jolly old booze-up with the warden.'

'Well let's do some patrolling ourselves,' I said.

'Hey? I don't know about you, but I'm bloody hungry. What's suddenly got into you anyway?'

'Okay, let's eat,' I replied. 'But I'm going out afterwards, even if you aren't.'

As we went to unload the Rover I noticed Chris had a look of baffled surprise.

After supper we learnt from the constable where the killing had taken place. A track, he said, passed right next to the spot.

'We might even see the lion coming there for a drink,' I said hopefully as we climbed into the Rover. 'If it really is a reserve lion, it shouldn't be frightened by a Land Rover.'

'If it goes there at all, it'll be in the early morning, not now,' Chris said as he started off. 'Anyway, we might as well take a look at the place, so's to seem intelligent when the general comes here tomorrow with his hangover.'

It was not long before we came to the watering-place. A shallow, temporary stream had been dammed for use of man and beast, and surrounded by bare trampled earth it looked desolate. In the headlights of the Rover we could see two paths disappearing into the surrounding bush; our eyes automatically followed the one heading north, which had led a woman to a nightmarish death. The idea of it silenced us both until Chris began fidgeting in his seat.

'What'll we do now?'

'Let's carry on a bit. This track goes to the reserve boundary, and we can look for spoor or something on the way.'

Chris drove on again. The sky had been clearing and an almost full moon was shining, making visibility good. We both felt adventurous and hoped something would turn up.

Simultaneously we shouted as the main beams picked up a lion trail on the road. The trail led from the south, then turned eastward into the bush on the same side as the dam. A quick look showed that one paw was damaged.

‘That’s him all right,’ Chris said.

‘I’d like to measure the imprints, it’ll give us some idea of his size.’ I felt which way the light breeze was blowing. ‘It should be safe because he’s gone up-wind.’

‘Okay, but don’t take long. I’ll mount guard.’

He hauled out a rifle and climbed onto the cab roof; there he sat with hands cupped to his ears.

Softly, after a few moments, he said, ‘I think someone’s having dinner out there.’

I listened too. One could just hear sporadic sounds coming with the breeze.

‘It could be him,’ I replied. ‘Maybe he’s got a goat – there were a couple loose a little way back.’

I climbed up beside Chris, trying to see through the darkness to where the lion must be. ‘He seems a big one, judging from the spoor.’

I felt intensely interested, intensely involved in what was happening. Yes, the warden had set us a problem. Why was this lion out here? A lot of things had to be fitted together: the wet conditions, the dispersal of game, the injured paw, cattle herders and the broken fence. Where were the remaining northern lions? Why were they not here too? Perhaps the whole natural economy of this waterless area was too weak to support the lion population, especially now that the game had spread away from water holes because of the rains. So the lions were being forced to open up new avenues of exploitation – or at least, this one, handicapped by an injured paw, had been driven to it.

A wave of eager, excited enthusiasm ran through me: why not start a proper study of lions in the reserve? The warden had implied that little was really known about their numbers, their movements. Well what about finding out?

What an idea! I would find out how they lived in the reserve, what they ate, where they hunted; try to see how they fitted into the reserve, and how they in turn affected it.

I pictured myself handing the chief a report on the status of lions in the reserve when he returned, with advice about the control of numbers.

'I've decided to make the study of lions in this reserve my official research project,' I announced excitedly. 'Blow the herons!'

'In that case we'll have to advertise for a replacement in a couple of weeks' time.' Chris's speciality was birds of prey, and he never could understand why people chose to study smelly mammals, especially those that are liable to eat you.

He added, 'You're off to a good start by having to shoot one of them.'

'Maybe the chief was right about overstocking, and this one should go in any case. But …' This magnificent animal, striving now to live under such difficulties. 'It's an awful thing to have to do, though.'

'Well, in nature when there are too many lions they simply have to starve, and eventually the hyaenas pull them apart. Shooting at least is quicker.'

'Yes. Bloody nature. Even the lions can't escape it.'

We sat in silence, feeling unsure whether this was the right moment to go in after the lion. Suddenly I caught sight of movement left of where the sound had been coming from.

'Look! There he goes, up towards the dam. Let's see what he's eaten.'

A jump down from the cab roof and we were in scrub, shining our torches on a tangle of skin, blood and bone.

Yes, a goat, the bare remains of a small goat. 'We'd better get to the dam and do something before someone else gets eaten,' Chris said. 'This kill amounts merely to a hors d'oeuvre.'

We hurried to the Land Rover, drove with as little noise as possible back to the dam and there in the moonlight a lion could plainly be seen at the water.

It eyed the vehicle for a moment, then went on drinking.

'Well,' I softly remarked, struck by this indifference, 'it certainly is a reserve lion.'

Chris rapped on the steering wheel. 'I suppose we ought to shoot it. The condition's ideal.'

'Yes, so let's not.'

'Hey? And what about the next person on his menu? There's still a chance of saving the other lions, but this one's obviously got a fixed idea about dining out. There's nothing we can do for him. I'm going to try driving closer.'

A cold wave of revulsion rose through me.

'But ...'

'Not quite sporting, old chap?' he asked with a hot-potatoes accent. 'Well,' he went on tersely, 'this isn't a time for sport. I'll draw the Rover broadside on, we'll get out on your side and try a simultaneous shot from behind the bonnet –' that was the extravagant sort of thing Chris would think of. 'You aim for the head.'

He drove to within easy shooting distance of the lion and signalled me out. I felt like rebelling.

'Come on,' he whispered. 'This is a job, not a conservation epic. Quick, or he'll go.'

I climbed out like an automaton and we took up position, steadying our rifles by leaning on the front mudguard. Suddenly the lion looked up at us, aware now of movement behind the vehicle. For a moment I thought it was going to bolt for cover, but it stood its ground, tail twitching threateningly upwards. It seemed to be making up its mind whether to charge or not.

Faintly Chris whispered, 'Steady, aim ...'

Crack!

The lion fell like a log, reduced suddenly to a formless heap indistinguishable from any other mound of earth beside the half-lighted dam.

A moment of keeping it covered, and we approached cautiously. Chris lifted a heavyish stone to throw when he got close enough while I stood by with rifle raised. But there was no response. The stone produced only a lifeless thud as it landed on the flank.

'That's the end of *his* problems,' Chris said a little unsteadily as he walked closer to shine a torch on wounds trickling blood from its head and chest.

'It's been fair shot to pieces,' he remarked as he bent over it. 'That's what you call a professional job; quick and clean.'

I discovered I was trembling all over. 'Well if it's got to be done, then I suppose you can look at it that way.'

'And what other way d'you want? A glorious climax to the hunt trying to track the poor bastard when it's disappeared wounded into the bush?'

I crouched beside the body and put a hand on its massive shoulder.

'I can tell you now that no other lions are going to need to get out of the reserve. Tomorrow I'm going to ask permission to put a dam wall like this across the north stream – with my own hands if necessary, and reinforce the fence. From now on I'm going to work like ...' yes, the chief had said it the morning I arrived, 'like a real maniac.'

Chapter Fourteen

Not long after the man-eater episode the game guards changed my name from the Fawn-who-sits-by-himself to the Fawn-who-walks-with-lions. Even routine work now was done with furious intensity, so that as much time as possible could be given to the lion study. A barrier was thrown across the north stream and did what I hoped: concentrate game for the lions. The fence in the Mkomo area was repaired and reinforced to keep the game in and the cattle out, and within a month it seemed that the remaining lions had a secure future – as secure, that is, as the bush itself allows.

All positive living. But, I wondered, was this the same as a positively insightful life? Positive living wasn't all there could be to Duma's mighty drive. Something was missing. The insightfulness that turned the lion hunt into a revelation: it seemed timeless then, but ordinary time had made it lose its clarity, immediacy, its state of seeing. It was during a spell when I felt the tug of this problem, some three months after the lion crisis, that Professor Bayes visited the reserve with two senior students to do some research on parasites. The professor needed no introduction to Chris, since Chris had been in his zoology classes. When it came to my introduction I was standing uneasily behind the reception desk in the office, thinking I was to meet a major source of Chris's views on life. But the person escorted by Chris into the office from the bright midday heat was kindly, unassuming; a calmly energetic man in his fifties with what struck me as a patriarchal beard. Greying hair fell as a thinning mane behind his head, deep blue eyes gazed straight into mine as I answered his questions. But it was a gaze I found reassuring.

'And what is your speciality?' the professor asked, quietly drawing up a chair to sit alongside the office desk.

'Well, I'm making a study of lions in this reserve.'

'Oh, yes?'

'But I haven't got very far. I've only been here about six months, and actually I only began studying them in earnest three months ago – the day I had to shoot one!'

Then I had to explain how such a thing could have been the start of my project. The professor seemed interested. Possibly he was surprised; maybe he expected someone with a tougher personality to become involved with lions. But he must have realised that I did not see lions that way. To me they were animals that suffered, that were as much exposed to the whims of nature as were the animals they preyed upon.

'While I'm here,' he said, 'perhaps you could fit in some time to show me your pets.'

Fit in some time? As I glanced at his work schedule laid out on the office desk, time seemed to be something he had overlooked: impossible to fit all that work into the week he planned staying here. He and his two students had come to study the internal parasites of buck, and the work schedule required a ranger every day to help with his collecting: shooting animals needed for dissection, transporting carcasses to the small reserve laboratory, then helping him mount and preserve his material. That came close to a twenty-four-hour day, since the animals were to be shot at night – daytime shooting makes the game link vehicles with trouble. In any case, shooting at night is easier, as any poacher knows.

'And you intend starting tonight, Professor?' I asked as I glanced up from his work schedule. I saw that Chris was down for the first night.

He gave a small nod, with a wry look. 'Yes, I start work tonight, if you can dignify as "work" anything attempted with our friend here.'

I met the professor's two students later in the day. They introduced themselves as Clive and Wendy, saying they wanted to see the reserve laboratory, a small building next to the garages. They had chosen a parasitology option as part of their course, they told me, and 'Prof's working us to death,' Clive groaned as we headed for the lab.

Wendy just gave a worried grin. Slender, earnest looking with light brown hair pulled back in a ponytail as if ready for business, she seemed less suited for the gory side of parasitology than the stocky, phlegmatic Clive. As we walked towards the lab she took quick, small steps, looking down at the ground just ahead of her more than at anything else.

I did not see much of them for the first two days. When it was my turn for night duty, only Clive came to select a bushbuck for shooting. Wendy hated seeing animals getting shot. I drove, and Nsundu came to do the shooting. It reminded me a little of my outing when Nsundu shot the lion cub.

Nsundu did not like night work and was disgruntled. As we drove down to the pans to pick out a buck, Clive was saying how great it was to be in the bush at night. And Nsundu said, 'You're not *in* the bush. You're sitting in a Land Rover, with a couple of rifles. If you really want to be out in the bush, then take off your shoes and start walking with no rifle – by yourself!'

'Hey?' It sounded as if Clive had not thought of it that way. 'You … you wouldn't survive the night, on your own.'

'Unless you spent it up a tree,' Nsundu remarked. 'At night you could be hit by a rhino, elephant, buffalo; eaten by lion;

anything. But at least you'd die knowing a little of what the real bush is like.'

I thought back to the time of discovery when the real bush revealed itself, the night of the lion hunt, but we said nothing until the lights of the Land Rover picked up a bushbuck ram, standing on its own near the pans. It seemed in poor condition.

Nsundu said, 'That one, it's got enough parasites for you.'

While the ram stood blinded by the headlights, Nsundu slipped silently out of the cab and with one shot reduced an animal to a heap of laboratory material.

Silently we loaded it into the vehicle, and headed back to camp.

The next morning it struck me that Wendy was visibly wilting. I was trying to get a stalled Land Rover going when I saw her come droopily across to me.

'I just want to get away from everything in that lab for a while,' she murmured. She leant against the Rover, looking dispiritedly into the engine compartment. 'I simply want to look at something clean, that doesn't smell.'

'Something clean?' I playfully lifted my oily hands off the carburettor to look at them.

'Oh …' She turned away, blinking a little. I hadn't realized how upset she was. 'I … suppose I'm stupid really, but …'

'Like to tell me what's wrong?' I said quietly.

She shrugged her shoulders despondently. 'Just that … well, I suppose it's simply all been too much, these few days.' She diverted her thoughts for a moment by running a finger over a big scratch on the Rover's side. 'I mean, everyone likes coming to a game reserve to look at the animals; they all look so beautiful out in the bush; but … well, you should see what a really parasite-infested animal looks like inside.'

The thought made her queasy. 'Such a mess, and I've been seeing it – smelling it – all morning. That poor thing you shot last night: its liver is like … rotten porridge. You've got a terrible infestation of liver flukes in this reserve.'

She shrugged her shoulders again. 'I … I don't know. Anyway, I'm just wasting your time. I don't usually go on like this.'

I laughed. 'Somehow, people *do* "go on like this" when they come here. Ask our camp superintendent – the first thing Sibanda said to me when I started work here was: there is something about the bush that opens and frightens the mind. You start asking questions, scary questions, and you become a philosopher – of a sort.'

'What …' Her eyes half met mine for the first time. 'What did it feel like, last night? I mean, killing that poor thing?'

'It was in bad condition – as you've seen from the parasites it was carrying. It wouldn't have lasted another night or so. Better a shot through the heart than being pulled apart alive by hunting dogs or hyaenas.'

That hardly cheered her up.

I tried to liven things. 'Did Clive tell you what Nsundu said to him while we were out? About having to take off his shoes and start walking, if he really wanted to be in the bush at night?'

She shook her head; perhaps Clive had been feeling a bit embarrassed about it. So I told her.

It didn't strike her as funny. 'Ooh!' She gave a little shudder. 'You'd be bitten by a snake or something. I'd die of fright.'

Her attention went back to running a finger along the scratch on the side of the Rover. 'Back home,' she said a little distantly, 'I joined a Gaia Club – Gaia is the earth goddess in Greek mythology, you know, and the Gaia idea is that the earth is a whole, almost living thing. Nature can be cooperative rather than competitive and aggressive, and … well, it's supposed all to fit together properly and to work, like your car is supposed to.'

I went back to checking the engine. 'Nature does work, in its own kind of way. If it doesn't work, then things get wiped out until it does. But I wonder what some of your club members would make of it if *they* were out in these African wilds, barefoot on their own at night. In most places the wild animals have been cleaned out, so now you can happily wander lonely as a cloud like Wordsworth through the tamed, impoverished countryside. But you can't do it here, where some of the world's great killers are still left.'

She pursed her lips. 'I've always thought of Gaia as a lovely, civilized idea. What you call "these African wilds" ...' Once more her finger trailed along the scratch on the Rover's side. Her eyes followed the movement dispiritedly. 'I don't know ... I just wish I'd never even started on this parasitology thing.'

'But surely, you must have come across all this in your undergrad years, before joining Prof's course.'

Eyes were still lowered. 'It's one thing to read about it, be lectured on it, see a few bottled specimens. But to see it actually in the raw like this, see what actually happens in nature ... can you understand that?'

I nodded. 'I've also had a taste of the difference between just thinking you know about something, and having to live with it. Maybe you couldn't have chosen a grimmer thing than parasites: so many different forms of life invading and exploiting other living things. It rubs your nose in the opportunist, no-holds-barred side of nature.'

As she went on gazing listlessly at the Rover's scratch, an evening scene with Duma at the big pan drifted through my mind: 'Look around you, what do you see?' he was asking. 'A pretty good free-for-all, isn't it?' A cut-throat game of snakes and ladders; and here, with parasites, the game had only one rule: that exploitation does not weaken the host so badly that the parasites can no longer make a living and slide towards extinction.

Her attention shifted from the metallic scratch to give me a half glance.

'Do you like being a ranger?'

'Why d'you ask?'

'I thought … well, when I think about it, I'd expect only insensitive types to do this kind of work.'

That brought back a picture of Cheryl, standing beside the desk, looking at what I was doing. 'You're so lucky,' she was saying, 'working here in this wonderful place.' And I did not feel too sure of that. It was an insecurity that let me say to Wendy, 'I actually understand how you feel.' Not the inner poise of Cheryl, ready to be taken beyond herself, or the wild abandon of the three Graces. I had to come to that through being frightened out of my mind while bogged down in a watercourse. And when I tried to tell Wendy about it, she didn't seem very reassured.

So I asked her, 'Then why did you choose parasitology as a subject? Was it to work with Prof. Bayes?'

The look was a bit more positive as her eyes rose fully to meet mine. 'He has a sense of direction away from the "no-holds-barred side of nature", as you called it. Just think of the awful things going on outside the reserve – the soaring human population, the destruction of land, all the political and economic mismanagement … even most parasites hit off a better conservation and survival deal than that. And as Prof keeps saying, we're just heading for *extinction* if we carry on this way, still so close to the animal state, still running on blind opportunism and exploitation. We need to understand the biology, the ecology of it all, so that we can get to something better. Gaia can become sick, and we're the worst parasites she's ever had to try to deal with. We've simply *got* to wake up.'

Now there was a more confident look. She fingered her pony tail and swung it forward over her shoulder. 'What Prof keeps telling us is the *one* positive thing that the whole university has to say about our future. He's truly inspirational when you hear him speak. But …' She could even afford a slight laugh now. 'Prof's going to head *me* for extinction if I don't get back to the lab! We've been so *busy* …'

And she walked fairly determinedly back to the lab.

Chapter Fifteen

I saw her again after lunch when I was due to make a routine check of the new north dam. A steady tourist attraction, now, the northern lions; drawn by the concentration of game round the dam they could be found without much trouble near their larder. The maintenance team even had to clear a site to cope with tourist cars and put up a small split-pole enclosure, a viewing stockade to allow people to walk about and have picnics without danger of attack.

Wendy's professor seemed to think she needed a break, so the two of them joined me for the dam, leaving Clive in the lab 'up to my nose in bloody guts,' as he put it. Some cars were parked there when we arrived. Once more I had to tell a group of visitors the story of how the dam came to be made, and why water is such a problem in this sandy area.

'But you don't have to worry about water around here,' one of the party said. 'You've got enough water running underground to supply a town.'

It was a man in his sixties, matter-of-fact, stooped a little and peering through his spectacles. I remembered hearing him discuss water pumps with Sibanda the day before; some kind of engineer, I supposed.

'How d'you know there's water here?' I asked him. 'By the vegetation?'

'No. The water's too far underground for that.' The look was still matter-of-fact, but just a little cautious now. 'I do it by – well …'

He pulled out of his pocket a little cone-shaped pendulum fitted to a nylon thread. It seemed to swing vigorously. 'Underground water, all right. If you like, I'll plot the course of the underground stream for you on a map. In a drought it might be handy to know about it.'

Wendy looked intrigued, but I heard her professor mutter 'Psychic claptrap. Dowsing they call it; I won't call it anything but delusion, deceitful conning.'

But the man looked honest enough. I asked, 'Can you really show me?'

'I could give it a shot.'

So back in the office, as I unfolded a map of the reserve on the desk he remarked, 'I suppose you won't believe all this, but here goes.'

He held the dancing pendulum over the map with one hand, with the other hand he drew a pencil line traced by the pendulum across the northern part of the reserve.

'Well, that's where it runs, the stream. It's about fifteen metres deep.'

He gave a slightly self-dismissive laugh to me and to Sibanda who had just come in with the professor. Sibanda watched the performance with interest.

'See where the line runs, Robbie?' he asked. 'Right under two of the guard posts.'

'Yes, that's where we have boreholes.'

'Is that so?' said the man-with-the-pendulum. 'That's interesting.' He blinked and nodded reassuringly. 'Well, you'll never run short of water up there. Worth bearing in mind, if your dam runs dry. Anyway, I must go off now and join the wife.'

I gave him a slightly bewildered look as he left, and said to Sibanda, 'How on earth did he work that out?'

Sibanda shrugged his shoulders. 'All I can tell you is that the chief would've liked this. This water divining or what you call it is just his thing.'

'I dare say it is,' remarked the professor drily, looking at the map. 'But if you want to know how your miracle man did it, he had only to be told that the two guard posts had boreholes, and his imagination could've done the rest.'

'He's not the first to tell us we have underground water there,' Sibanda replied. 'Other people sense the same thing.'

'Sense it?' the professor asked caustically.

'That's right.' There was a trace of impatience in Sibanda's voice. 'They don't see it, they don't hear it, they *feel* it –' he waved a finger above him – 'in the mind.'

The professor walked towards the door. Looking round bleakly at Sibanda he said, 'And you expect me to take that seriously?'

'Well I can tell you why we have the guard posts where they are – because the chief got someone else like that on the job to find water.'

'Someone who was good at finding money!'

'How d'you mean?'

'I suppose it never occurred to your chief that the person first found where water had been discovered running outside the reserve, and then successfully guessed where it ran just inside the reserve. Clever. No doubt he was paid handsomely for his services.'

He walked impatiently out of the office without saying anything more.

Sibanda watched him go. His head was tilted thoughtfully to one side.

'Funny, isn't it?' he said as he gazed after him.

'What's funny?'

'The way people like him take this kind of thing – divining, psychic or what-you-call-it. He'd sooner argue the backside off a donkey than want to accept it.'

'Well he had a reason for not accepting it – that person might've known about it from boreholes outside the reserve.'

'Reason?' Sibanda was becoming impatient again. 'A reason? Your clever professor had no reason at all. Can't you see – he just took a wild guess, and then pretended it was right. If you really want to know, when we sank those boreholes, there wasn't another drilling this side of the horizon. Eah! Those people –' he glanced after the professor; 'their name is bigger than their brain.'

I was getting roused too. 'He's a leading scientist in …'

'You really think the man who came in just now knew about those guard posts?'

'I … I don't know.'

'Why don't you go and ask your professor? He seems to know everything.'

'All right then, how do *you* think he did it?'

Sibanda grinned. 'At least I've been with the chief long enough to be careful about saying: that's impossible because all the big scientists say it can't happen. Last year we had someone who could find minerals – went round with a thing on a string also. He said we had a small ore deposit just south of the river.'

'And so?'

'The chief found he was dead right – so he threw an exclosure fence round the place so no-one would discover it. He doesn't want people wrecking up the reserve with their mines.'

'But if that's a good way of prospecting, why don't you hear more about it?'

'Just think about your professor, and you'll know why! I just say that kind of thing *does* work – that's why we have the guard posts where they are. Why don't you go and ask the pendulum man how *he* thinks it works?'

'Rats!'

The whole thing seemed queer – in some way even distasteful. 'Get on with something sensible,' I said to myself, remembering that my next job was to help Prof. Bayes in the lab. Something sensible: a heave out of the office chair and – avoiding another glance at Sibanda – I headed myself through the door towards the lab. 'Something sensible,'

I muttered to myself, the job of preparing blood smears for the prof, spreading drops of blood from the bushbuck killed last night over the glassy surface of microscope slides.

At least, it seemed perfectly sensible as I settled on a stool against the lab bench. Wendy was there too, examining slides under a microscope. She didn't find this type of work too bad, looking for blood parasites. And as I started to smear red blood drops across the slides I said to the professor, 'You certainly meet some odd people coming to this reserve. That water diviner or whatever you call him ...'

'Unfortunately you don't only meet them here,' the prof interrupted, looking up from his microscope. 'Do you know that only the other day, someone living near the university was in court on a charge of giving medical diagnoses with the use of a pendulum? And the incredible thing was that the quack's patients were prepared to declare in court that his diagnoses were accurate! It just shows how people with a taste for the supernatural, psychic chicanery, can be fooled.'

'But – but in actual fact were his diagnoses really not accurate?'

The professor turned impatiently back to his microscope. 'How on earth could they be? He used his clients' saliva as some sort of sample, and how can a drop of spit tell you what's wrong with a person? The way people still yield to superstition is horrifying – one would almost think we were still in the middle of some dark age.'

Dark age; yielding to superstition. I put down the slide I had smeared with blood and looked at it blankly. A question was forming somewhere in my head; a question I did not really want to be there.

Exactly who was being superstitious?

Was it people who were prepared to testify in court about what they had experienced, or was it a professor who said flatly that it couldn't happen, that it couldn't be experienced?

I gazed at the rows of microscope slides, glassy and stained. Sibanda's question came back to me: 'Why don't you go and ask that man how he thinks it works?' Blood smears ... I had heard that someone had just been caught in the reserve with a blood-smeared hunting spear. He also had a spade for digging bulbs. The bulbs were used for medicine. Outside the reserve the medicinal plants had been exploited to extinction except for a small nursery that Duma had been able to establish, but still there was plundering of the reserve and its store of plant life. The charge against the man for digging protected plants was bad, but worse, what about the hunting spear stained with blood? Had he been poaching animals as well?

He could not be charged with poaching because there was no concrete evidence. The stains came from slaughtering a goat, he claimed, and there was no hair of any game animal stuck to his spear to prove him wrong. Supposing Mr Clark, the man with the pendulum, could do the same thing as the man who was up in court. It was a kind of diagnosis: could he tell whether the blood came from a goat or from game, whether the case was worth pursuing or not?

That would be a test. Sibanda's challenge: why don't you go ...

'I, I've got a poaching case to deal with,' I said rather awkwardly to the professor. 'I think I'll have to hurry off now.'

So I left, and 'Sibanda's challenge,' I kept thinking to myself as I walked to the Clarks' hut with the hunting spear in my hand, otherwise another half of me would have won: 'Idiot, get right back to those slides!'

Mr Clark, on the little verandah of his hut, had just finished a cup of tea and was methodically cleaning a camera lens before packing it in its case. 'Just call me Jim,' he said when I introduced myself again, saying I had something to ask him.

'Well …' His look at me after hearing my story was frank. 'I've never done exactly this sort of thing before; but there's a real need for it to work, isn't there? And a need makes all the difference.'

Out came the pendulum from his pocket.

'Got a bit of paper?' he asked.

I tore a sheet from the notebook I carried with me. He placed it on the small verandah table, writing the words 'goat' and 'game' with a look of abstraction. Then next to it he placed the spear, holding the pendulum above a stain where blade and handle joined. A finger of his free hand went from 'goat' to 'game' and back again; his look was becoming puzzled.

'That's odd,' he said. 'I don't pick up a thing. How old is the stain?'

'The man was caught this morning. And it's a new spear – see how clean the shaft is. It's probably been used the first time today.'

Jim held his pendulum over the blade again.

His look now had become grim. With an unwilling gesture he added the word 'man' to his list.

The pendulum circled vigorously, clockwise, over the stain.

'See; that means "yes",' he quietly remarked. 'I suggest you go quickly and find out what's been happening.'

'There's no report of anyone being injured. Would you like to come with me to find what's happened?' I thought I should at least test his faith in himself before starting on what looked like a senseless goose chase. 'The poacher was caught trying to get through the southern boundary fence, near a stand of bulbs he was digging.'

'Rather! And take a first aid kit. I've done a bit of first aid, so I might even be of some use.'

Without telling anyone – not even Sibanda – where I was going, we climbed into a Land Rover to head down to the raided plants near the boundary.

Driving along a twisty track through the bush, I tried to keep my mind a blank; but I could not shake out a picture of Dakwa, one of the oldest game guards. He was supposed to be on foot patrol at the southern boundary, but no-one had made contact with him when the poacher was caught at the fence. Yet patrols hardly worried if Dakwa didn't show up. He was partial to drink, and one day, they said, even the hyaenas that ate him would get drunk.

Soon we reached the stand of plants beside the track, short green pointed leaves poking from the ground. There were signs of digging for bulbs, footprints heading for the reserve fence, and prints of a guard heading towards the nearest guard camp. There was blood mixed with the guard's prints. I cupped my hands to my mouth.

'Dakwa!'

No reply. Jim soberly regarded the blood trail as though he were examining a burst water pipe. 'My guess,' he said, 'is that you should chase after that man fast.'

We scrambled back into the Rover. A short way down the track we saw a figure collapsed on the roadside.

'Dakwa!' I shouted leaping out of the cab again. 'For God's sake!'

The man was too exhausted to stand, and one glance at his chest showed where blood on the spear could have come from.

'Hau!' Dakwa weakly called back in Zulu. 'The Fawn-who-walks-with-lions; the Fawn-who-comes-to-those-who-are-dying! Great Magic-man! There is a murderer in the reserve. He tried to kill me as I caught him stealing bulbs.'

Quickly Jim examined the bleeding wound. 'Lucky the spear didn't enter his chest,' he calmly remarked. 'Wouldn't have lasted long if that had happened.'

'He wouldn't have lasted long in any case, if you hadn't got this rescue party going.'

Jim applied a pad to the wound. 'Well ...' He sounded matter-of-fact. 'It's not the first time that dowsing has saved a life.'

'But how does it work?'

Wide-eyed, he stopped bandaging for a moment to stare at me. 'How does it work? Look, if I could tell you how it works, I'd be a century ahead of my time!'

Then kneeling beside Dakwa at the side of the bush-walled track he went on bandaging in his methodical way.

'All I know,' he muttered half to himself, 'is that it *does* work, especially like now, when there's a real *need* for it to work.'

With Dakwa securely bandaged we helped him into the Land Rover. What he had to say left no doubt that the man caught with the spear had done the stabbing.

'But ...' As we started along the dusty track for camp I found myself glancing round to see if Dakwa really was there, to be sure it actually had happened. 'But it simply doesn't make sense.'

Jim shrugged his shoulders, blinking pensively. 'There'd be some hope of it starting to make sense if more people were prepared to investigate it properly. It's mental, you see; the mind has to be tuned for it to work, fine tuned with the right kind of question to get the right kind of answer. Yet, your scientists can't cope with the mental side of things – think of that professor. "Psychic claptrap," I overheard him say.'

His look had become gloomy. 'Also, there has to be a no-nonsense *need* for it to work, not just some clever experiment.

And how many scientists could really know and understand that?'

A gloomfilled gaze out of his window was followed by, 'If you ask me, I think we're right bang in a dark age – the worst ever, because we choose to think that we've emerged from what we like to call the Dark Ages.'

I didn't feel like taking the matter any further. I had knocked on the door of what seemed a mere curiosity and had been faced with a weird, gaping chasm opening up in the fabric of what I took to be ordered reality. Already I was trying to close the hole with forgetfulness, one part of me pretending to the other that it hadn't really happened. Yet the last meeting in Duma's study kept coming back to me: 'All you do is stop on the established road, and walk a few paces off it,' he was saying. 'Then you'll see what a crappy little track that established road is – you actually *see* it.'

I had been taken a few paces off the settled road, yet quickly scrambled back, changing the subject to water pumps for the rest of the trip to camp.

As we drove through the camp gates I said, 'Well, Dakwa has a lot to thank you for. And I suppose I should thank you also. This has been quite a shake-up.'

Jim looked impassive. 'You're a biologist, aren't you?'

'A kind of one, maybe, in a practical sense.'

'Then you might find it useful to remember what another biologist, J.B.S. Haldane, thought. He suspected that the Universe is not only queerer than we suppose, but queerer than we actually *can* suppose. Please, for your own enlightenment, remember that science is as much an expression of our limitations as of our abilities. Therefore, a scientist has no business to dismiss areas of study such as dowsing, parapsychology, simply because they "don't make sense". Of *course* they don't make sense in science's present limitations and its downgrading of mind. But that doesn't mean to say that such things don't exist, or that they're not worth trying to study.'

We had now drawn up at the office. There was a look of preoccupation on Jim's face as he helped Dakwa out of the Land Rover. He seemed deeply moved by what he had just been saying, and stooped in concentration he walked wordlessly back to his hut.

When I joined the professor and Wendy in the lab late that afternoon I found it difficult to focus on preparing more microscope slides.

Wendy noticed.

'What's on your mind?' she asked. 'Something just happened?'

But I didn't feel like telling her with Prof. Bayes there.

Chapter Sixteen

Lights were on in the lab after supper. I thought Wendy might still be preparing blood slides. But as I got to the door, the talking and laughing sounded more like a party. Wendy was there, but also Clive and Chris. They had been at university together, and there they were, 'D'you remember the time …?', Clive and Chris each with a can of beer.

I turned to leave, thinking I would merely be intruding, but, 'Have a beer,' Clive shouted. 'Smuggled this in with all the preservative. And now it's time *we* got pickled.'

'Only one night left after this, thank goodness,' Wendy said.

'Not the best few days of your life?' I asked as I was passed a can.

She gave a little squirm. 'Well, at least now I know what kind of job to avoid.'

'Tough time,' Clive said, taking another gulp of beer. 'But was it Prof or the worms that were worse?'

'Where is he,' I asked Clive, 'your prof?'

'Having dinner with the camp superintendent. Otherwise we'd be out in the bloody bush again.'

'Hence the party,' Chris observed.

That led to a round of beer drinking, except Wendy; she had a cool drink. She looked at me quizzically. 'Tell me, when you came in this afternoon, you looked so … well, puzzled, shocked. Had something happened?'

'Certainly had. But that's a long story.'

Clive started laughing. 'A contact of yours in the rhino horn business, who didn't show up?'

'Wrong,' Chris said. 'It's the ivory we keep in the guard posts.'

This didn't seem a good time to talk about Jim Clark, but, 'Pulled in a game guard today, stabbed,' I said.

Wendy screwed her face. 'That must've been – *awful.* No wonder you couldn't settle down in the lab again.'

'Well, at least the guard was picked up in time. He was on his own, and could've died otherwise.'

'How did you find him?' Clive asked.

'Tourist found him.'

That made Clive laugh again. 'So tourists actually do some good sometimes?'

'This guy; well ...' I looked round at them. 'Well, you won't believe it, but ...' So the story came out.

When it was finished, Chris was the first to comment.

'Biggest load of crap I've ever heard. Duped, that's what you were.'

Clive took a lighthearted swig of beer. 'They say that people *do* go wacky in the bush. Can't blame them, after the few days I've had.'

Wendy looked thoughtful. 'I know a couple of people ... they use a pendulum to test food. They say you can find out if something has gone off, or doesn't agree with you, simply by swinging a pendulum over it.'

Chris's expression had turned sour, but Clive was amused. 'Let's try it out! Who's psychic? Here's some beer and – what? formalin – *terrible* stuff. Okay, which one is not too bad for us? Where's a pendulum?' He searched the bench and settled on a key tied by string to a label. 'Right.' He concentrated hard as he let the key hang over a bottle of formalin, then a beer can.

He had to say, as he returned to the formalin bottle, 'Hey, it *does* swing differently, sort of. Here, Wendy, you try it.'

With her there was a bigger difference in the swing over the two. But as Clive said, 'Wouldn't like to stake my life on it. You try, Rob.'

There was even less success with me.

He handed the key to Chris, but Chris, still looking sour, waved it to one side.

'Come on,' said Clive brightly, 'an extra beer for whoever does best.'

'Stuff it,' Chris said getting up. 'If you guys can't think of anything more intelligent to do, then I'm going to bed.'

For a couple of seconds there was baffled silence. Wendy looked at her watch. 'I suppose we all should go to bed, really. Prof wants us early tomorrow.'

So the beer was finished with little more talking, and we walked off to the tourist huts, first to see Wendy home. Wendy walked beside me, Clive and Chris a few paces behind.

'That ... that thing that happened to you today,' she said softly. 'I thought it was rather wonderful.'

'D'you really think that kind of thing can happen?'

'It *did* happen, didn't it?'

'Just as I told you. But it's no good telling Chris.'

'Well,' she said, 'if he believes it to be impossible – completely wrong in some way – what can you expect?'

'But – he's supposed to be a scientist, open minded and all that.'

She gave a little laugh. 'Chris a scientist? Chris is Chris, first and foremost. I suppose that's how we all are, really; scientists are just people, and how many people are truly open-minded? Even Prof is like that in some ways: dogmatic, with pet hates – you heard what he said at the dam about psychic claptrap. I think your man with the pendulum saw the truth about scientists very clearly.'

We had arrived at her hut.

'It's funny,' she said as we paused at her door, 'but it's the intolerant, unscientific side of Prof that seems to rub off so easily on people like Chris, the sort of clever-clever people. That performance of his this evening ... and yet Prof can be so inspirational, like I told you. Anyway, don't get put off by those people. What happened to you today … it really was very wonderful. And …' I felt her give my hand a light squeeze, 'thank you so much for the talk we had this morning. It helped keep me going, even if it was a little frightening.'

I gave her a reassuring squeeze back. Clive and Chris had caught up by this time, and as we left her hut there was an abrupt 'What was she saying?' from Chris.

I did not feel like telling him.

Chapter Seventeen

Professor Bayes, busy in the laboratory next day, kept dropping hints about shooting a lion as well as other game. 'So many parasite life cycles get completed in the gut of a carnivore,' he muttered, 'and we know so little about it all – especially about how your lions fit into the picture.'

But the best I could offer was to take him on a lion-watching trip at sunrise next day, the day of his leaving. He had been too busy in the lab to do much sightseeing, so he seemed interested, and, 'Perhaps while we're out, you might manage to back the Rover into a lion or two by accident,' he said hopefully, 'and we can take them to the lab.'

In the fresh breeze of dawn next day I stood at the camp fence with hands cupped to my ears. I felt almost sure that south of the camp we would see a kill.

I could have expected the professor to be up in time; he had enough drive for that. But so early in the morning he did not seem to be in very good shape. He was a little morose as he clambered into a Land Rover I had waiting for him.

As we drove out of camp he muttered gloomily about the lack of personal incentive among his undergraduates. 'They could all do with a couple of years of your sort of work. I imagine you've come up against quite a lot in the time you've been here.'

'Yes. In fact … in fact so much that I don't even have the faith of a missionary's son any longer – and Chris hammered quite a few wedges into the cracks during that process.'

'Chris?' He started to look faintly amused. 'Well, Chris has all the answers – except to his exam questions, of course.'

He turned to look at the rising sun.

'That's a sight! I suppose I've forgotten what a pollution-free sunrise looks like, stuck away in my grimy old ivory tower.' He was brightening up. 'Lots of game about, too. Look at all those zebra!'

'I'm pretty sure we'll be coming to a kill soon.'

'Oh? That would be interesting. Yes …' He became reflective again, but as he turned to me I saw another flicker of amusement. 'Yes; Chris Pickerell. Mind you, a shake-up at your time of life is all to the good. Once you've outgrown the stage of – you can say, intellectual breast-feeding, then you've got to …'

'Look, there's the kill!'

I wasn't sure if I should have broken into his musings, but he sounded pleased. 'Right, they've bagged a zebra!'

As we drove close he craned forward, trying to see what parts of the zebra they were eating. 'Well, there you have it: the family taking its daily dose of parasites,' he muttered. 'When next a lion dies – please – I want you to take gut samples. There must be at least three species of tapeworm in this reserve, and heaven knows how many roundworms.'

'Perhaps not what the tourists want to hear. But even that is a bed-time story compared to the things that go on here in the bush.'

'And did your religion not help you?'

My only response was a kind of wince.

He leaned slightly towards me, looking interested. 'So then, a caring person like you; is all you could do … rage at your god for creating the array of hurt and death that you see here every day, every night?'

'In the end, about the only thing I found right in the prayer book was, "In the midst of life we are in death." And it didn't take Chris long to prove that death is death, nothing beyond.'

The professor gazed at the bloodied scene. 'Yes. In the midst of life ...' He turned to me with a slight nod. 'Mind you –' his look was more questioning – 'if the idea of a life after death is merely an empty dream, then isn't it better to be shaken out of it? And of *course* it's merely a dream: consciousness is the result of information-processing systems generated in the brain. So, there can be no consciousness when the brain ceases to function at death, can there?'

A hand passed thoughtfully over his beard. 'But think of this: do we value a bowl of flowers any less because tomorrow they'll be withered and gone? Then why should we think differently of ourselves? Why degrade the beauty, the vital responsibility of being alive? Why not look for meaning simply where you can expect to find it: in the sheer business of living, here and now? Where else, I ask you?'

He turned back to face the lions with an assured nod.

'And does that not lead to betterment of living? We need have no faith save in the capabilities and possibilities of man, faith that man is rational enough to see – even if it takes time and bitter experience – that life can be tolerable only if lived according to what are the plain, unadorned facts around us and within us. And don't think that means some dry, dehumanizing programme. Quite the opposite – the unswerving quest for truth exercises a quality of mind that in action dispenses justice, in social relationships breeds consideration and respect, in artistic creation gives veracity and boldness, and in the affairs of government – why,' he said pointedly, 'just think what effect a real concern for facts and truthfulness would have on the lie-ridden jungle of politics and diplomacy.'

The professor gazed at the lions with almost unseeing eyes, deeply absorbed by what he was saying.

'Yes, such is the possibility of man, one that our species at this very moment is in a position to embark on, a transformation as momentous as the transformation from the non-living to the living. A new creation. And –' his open face turned to me again – 'isn't that something really meaningful to engage oneself in, rather than to go about engrossed in a snivelling concern for personal immortality?'

He seemed to think there was no need for an answer; he turned to take photographs out of the window. When he was finished I said to him, 'Shall we drive across to that pan over there to watch the hippo? This lion pride will probably end up there too.'

'Yes, that's an idea.' He was looking eagerly about him.

I backed away from the remains of the kill, to begin a slow drive towards the pan.

The professor turned to me. 'I'd like to see the results of your work on these animals. When do you plan to write your first report?'

'I want to have a report ready for when John Duma comes back.'

'Hmm. Maybe you could send me a copy as well. Tell me, have you ever thought of going to university?'

'Why yes! I've done more than think about it. But I've no money of my own, and I couldn't get a scholarship because of uneven school results – spent too much time on my favourite subjects; lost out on the others. I suppose I wouldn't be accepted in any case.'

The professor gave a sceptical grunt. 'You can take it from me that school results are of limited value when it comes to telling us who's going to be a good research worker, and who is not. There are better ways of judging a man's potential than to look at his school record. Yes, I'd be interested to see your report.'

'Well, I'll send you a copy, Professor, but I'm afraid it won't be very good.'

'No need to worry about perfection yet. At the moment it's the promise that counts. By the way, when will Duma return?'

'In about four months' time.'

I pulled up the Land Rover for a moment to watch a couple of giraffe, gracile and lofty.

'Did you see much of Duma before he left?' asked the professor.

'A lot, but I arrived only a month before his leaving.'

'Did he tell you much about his interests?'

'Not much, but he seems to hold some rather unconventional ideas. Do you know him, Professor?'

He grunted. 'Met him at a conference recently. Gave an interesting paper on wildlife and rural people, but at a pub afterwards he was talking appalling rubbish about witch-doctors. What d'you think of his … what you call "unconventional ideas"?'

'I heard him talk about them only once – the day of his leaving. I imagine Jim Clark's map dowsing would have interested him; he seems to believe that people can somehow see things at a distance – I don't know – something like that.'

'Yes,' repeated the professor ironically, 'something like that.'

He shifted in his seat to face me squarely.

'You know, Robert, since you're setting foot on a scientific career, I feel there may be one or two things to consider. I'm certainly not one to discourage honest investigation into anything that yields itself to the rigours of scientific investigation and analysis; but to occupy oneself with things that are frankly occult is to me quite another matter. Now Duma is certainly a first-rate biologist – you must not misunderstand me on that. Yet he also toys with things that I believe a modern scientist would find time-wasting, and less than helpful for his career. I feel it's not my business to say more than that, but remember what I've just said: the path of reason is narrow, and there are many tempting by-ways that may seem easier of access, and evidently more attractive to some individuals. But these by-ways can only lead mankind as a whole into a morass. The stable foundations of modern science were not built above this morass for nothing.'

The giraffe had moved away by this time, so I drove on, thinking there was little point in mentioning Duma's contempt for the Establishment's 'path of reason', or Jim Clark's views on scientists. But now it was time to think of something else. 'We're coming to the biggest pan,' I said. 'This is our real showpiece.'

It was the pan that the chief and I had visited the morning which now seemed so far back in time, my first morning with him as a ranger. The spreading water-lilies, the reeded margin, the surrounding lawn of grass under the fever-trees; the whole scene was as fresh as when I saw it on that morning. Yes, even the call of the fish-eagles; these things one's memory can retain only imperfectly, so they will always appear fresh and new.

'What a paradise!' exclaimed the professor.

I drew up to the edge of the pan, near a group of hippo. The professor reached for the door handle. 'Can't we get out for a while?'

I smiled and without a word pointed to some movement in the water a little way along the margin.

'What's going on there?' he asked. 'Why, a buck floating in the water – oh! … it's being eaten by crocodiles!'

'We can get out, Professor, but I'd sooner you stayed here. In any case, we'll see more game if we keep under cover.'

'Yes, you're quite right.'

He gazed with a mixture of fascination and revulsion at the slow, deliberate feasting. A crocodile would grasp a piece of carcass, then tug and rotate till a mouthful was torn off. It would disappear, and another would take its place. I heard him mutter, 'Yet amongst all this carnage, still I would say of this place, what a paradise.' And more loudly, 'Here there is no malice.'

I dared to say, ‘That is why I could be hesitant to leave this place for what I hear is the malice you find in universities, among scientists.’

‘You have a point,’ he replied. ‘But it’s people like you who might be able to help with that.’

I looked at him with the unspoken, How?

‘Think of this,’ he said. ‘It’s a matter of ecology, largely, and you are in a better position than many to understand that. The concern people show today for the environment, human and otherwise, it’s largely thanks to modern science, to the awareness science has given us of the interrelatedness, the ecology, the interdependence of things. Our age needs scientists who carry that insight forward. Whatever the detractors of science may like to say, don’t blame the scientific spirit for the disasters that the politicians, the generals and the developers have heaped upon this world; look to people’s lust for power and the devouring consumerism of our mad economy, not to scientific understanding. And that is where you can come in; individual scientists themselves are not blameless in corrupting the ideals of science, so we need people who can look beyond their own egotistical interests, beyond mere self, to what, yes, the pureness of these wilds can teach you.’

The nod he gave was so emphatic as almost to be a lunge.

‘We should develop scientific ideals and so direct the rational control of our circumstances towards a new mode of existence, a new creation – ’ he gestured to the stilled pan – ‘as pure as this one. Is there not a role for you there? Frail and floundering though we still are, what infinite scope, what endless possibilities stretch before us if we take up true responsibility. And even now, those who hold this great ideal and vision before them can rise above their tribulations and even their ultimate personal extinction; for they are pioneers of a new creation, and their works shall truly live after them.’

He looked out across the open pan as though addressing the whole natural world, deeply moved by what he was saying.

'The alternatives are clear. Either mankind adopts scientific, evolutionary humanism and goes forward to a new mode of existence, a new creation in rational harmony with all life, or else we continue to be bogged down in greed, destruction, fear, oppression, superstition, ultimately to end in ignominious extinction; merely another of the many evolutionary lines that could not sustain itself. And what stupendous potential would be lost! We have reached a stage of intelligence when our existence need no longer proceed through brute natural selection and survival of the fittest; our task is fitting our fellow beings to survive, by rational selection of true knowledge, harmonious action, and fruitful ideas. And with the steady accumulation of intellectual treasures and physical control, we set ourselves on a course that soon disappears beyond our most sanguine expectations. Who could decline a role in this new creation?'

I found myself moved. I felt as stirred as the professor. Sitting next to him, feeling the power of his idealism, I wanted to … yes, 'truly inspirational' is how Wendy put it – I leapt out of the Land Rover and began bellowing at the hippos. They bellowed back. Then I cupped my hands to my mouth and yodelled the call of the fish-eagle, leaning backwards and waving my body.

'Good God!' exclaimed the professor. 'What *is* going on?'

Chapter Eighteen

The professor's party left later in the day. As we watched the university minibus lumber off, Chris muttered, 'Having him around was as bad as being in a continuous bloody practical exam. Now I'm going to lie up for a few days.'

Hardly like an exam, I thought – more like seeing a vast museum display that was strangely put together: the professor's soaring temple to reason, embodying a faith, hope and charity that could bring salvation to emerging man; yet below ran cracks of unredeemed ape-man, intolerant, tribalizing facts and doing all the things the faith spoke out against. I wondered, did this temple differ very much from any other religion man had put together?

And so, as we waved the professor and his students goodbye, the question still hung in the dust thrown up behind them: what is one to believe?

But then, do you have to believe anything?

'You have the chance …' Duma had said this at an exclosure a long time ago, 'you have the chance of cutting adrift and being given the freedom to have a lot of fun exploring life and living.' To take that chance was at the time the last thing I wanted. All I wanted was to keep moored, tightly moored; but now after the Clark and Bayes episodes I wondered, was there really anything left to be moored to?

'You have the chance …' Yes! Now I could see, I could feel – and in a sudden excitement I could even relish – that now there seemed no mooring posts, no beliefs, no creeds, no doctrines, fences, left standing in the living waters all about me. That had all been swept away. All that ever could be left after what had happened in the last seven months was a simple state of being – a being that is a sharing, a partaking; in some obscure way a state of being that is also a state of knowing – yes, Jim showed me that connection. A state of mind that brings things to the mind. Something glimpsed during the lion hunt – the emptiness that opened into boundless beyond-thingness, infinite relatedness. So then there simply was nothing else to become now but one who sang with the fish-eagles, one who walked with lions, who swept across the hot plains like the rush of wind before a storm. In a Land Rover stripped down to its barest essentials I would be out before the rest of the camp had stirred, coursing endlessly through the bush with notebook in hand, recording, thinking, exulting; a part of the wilds that had become reflectively aware. The meaning, the purpose of life had become to experience life, in as unlimited a way as possible. Yes, the professor was right: 'Why not look for meaning simply where you can expect to find it: in the sheer business of living, here and now?'

Perhaps it was the nearest I could come to the abandon of the ecstatic three Graces.

The nine months of Duma's leave were quickly running out. 'Robbie,' Sibanda kept saying, 'you should push off to your folks for a couple of days – you know what it'll be like once the chief gets back: no time for anything.'

'What would I be like hanging round the mission with nothing to do there, and everything to do here?' was my reply. 'My parents haven't paid their annual visit, anyway. *This* is the place for us to see each other; here.'

Which is how it worked out. For a few days I found myself having to host my parents in the reserve.

Sibanda threw a dinner for them the evening they arrived. There was plenty of fun, with Sibanda taking a dig at me whenever conversation flagged.

'The lions have never had it so good,' he said as we left the table for cooler air on the verandah. 'Just now you'll see him clear off because it's got round to their feeding time.'

Martha laughed. 'Eah! What's on their menu for tonight, Robert?'

'Why,' said my father, 'that sounds like the story of the tourists who once asked Duma if they could go with him when he went to feed the elephants.'

'Well I can imagine what sort of answer the chief gave them,' I said, 'and you're all heading for the same treatment from me!'

'You hear that?' asked Sibanda. 'He's been getting a big lip since he's been here, hasn't he? Anyway, the chief just told them he was sorry but he'd run out of buns. Come on, Robbie, you can help hand round the coffee and get us fixed up before you put your lions to bed.'

'You aren't going out tonight, are you?' asked my mother.

'Oh, he needn't worry about small things like talking to parents,' my father said. 'I think we'll be turning in early, in any case.'

My mother looked dubious. 'I only hope he knows what he's doing out in the bush at night. *I* think it's very dangerous.'

'Well if I haven't found out how to look after myself by now, I might just as well get eaten. Why don't you come out with me?'

'Good heavens no!'

'By George, I'll go with you!' exclaimed my father. 'There shouldn't be anything my son can do that I cannot!'

'Oh no you don't,' my mother retorted. 'Whatever Robert's got on his lions' menu, it's not going to be you! You just stay put.'

'I jolly well am going out with him.'

'It'll simply be a short run in the Land Rover,' I remarked with superior calm. 'It'll be very dull, I can assure you.'

'What d'you have to do tonight anyway?' Sibanda asked.

'I just want to see if the southern pride have left their kill. They took a young hippo near the pans – that's very unusual.'

My father looked at his watch. 'How long will you be?'

'Not long. I was up the whole of last night; I'm due for some sleep tonight.'

So that evening my father came with me down to the floodplain.

We travelled slowly. The bush had become cool, still, dewy, almost an underwater scene as light from a full moon marked out the space between shrubs and trees. Game stood darkly etched or faintly luminous in open spreads of grass, and I drove with parking lights only, not to dazzle the animals ahead or blind ourselves to the scenes on either side. Now and then we would pause to let a nightjar fly up out of our way, and once it was even a leopard padding along the sandy track ahead of us that made us stop.

There was no mistaking our arrival at the floodplain. The croaks, honks and whistles of massed choruses of frogs in reeds, in trees, on lily pads and sandy beaches almost drowned our talking. My father had been chatting the whole way – not with my co-operation, for talking seemed out of place in a night ride through the bush. Also, I had tried to cut down conversation in case it came round to the topic dropped ever since our exchange of letters after the hailstorm and the shooting of the cub: the matter of religion. This subject, I felt, was better left alone.

'I must say …' My father was still talking as we drew up at the skull and scattered bones that once had been a young hippo. 'I wouldn't have liked to see this kill taking place – lions wouldn't be able to bring down a hippo in a quick, clean way, I imagine.'

The lions had disappeared, and the remains were now in the final stages of disintegration: a couple of jackals were picking up scraps. They refused to leave even when we pulled right up to the spot.

‘Well, I’d say that’s that,’ my father remarked as he gazed through the windscreen at the tattered wreckage. ‘It’s a good thing there are more hippo where that one came from.’

‘Making Providence do some work?’ I asked, unable to check the remark before it slipped out. ‘Anyway,’ I added hastily, ‘we can get back to camp now – I’m not going round after the southern pride tonight.’

There was a more thoughtful look on my father’s face as I backed away from the kill and began to drive off.

‘You know,’ he said once we were moving, ‘I’ve often wondered what you made of that letter I wrote soon after you came here, when you seemed so troubled. I never heard anything more about it.’

‘Well, I didn’t really have anything more to say.’

‘Why? Were you still troubled?’

‘At the time, yes. Awfully.’

‘And now?’

‘Perhaps now you’d say I’m in *real* trouble. *I* wouldn’t say that; but – I don’t think it would help to argue about it.’

A touch of humour in his voice came as a surprise. ‘Who suggested arguing about anything, Robert? But at least you can tell me where you stand now. Don’t you think that would interest me? And don’t you think that I too have had to ponder long and hard after that letter I wrote?’

So above the chorus of frogs I told the story of how my beliefs had collapsed, what happened during the lion hunt; then, best as I could, described the meeting with Professor Bayes and the twist Jim Clark had given it.

‘And so,’ I ended, ‘you see why I said earlier, perhaps you think I’m now in real trouble.’

He paused a moment before saying, ‘I wonder … perhaps it is rather *you*, Robert, who think that *I* am the one in trouble, sitting out there on the rocks, blissfully unaware of the tide of science and reason that is steadily coming in to swamp all my nonsense.'

I laughed. 'Well, you said it …'

'And I suppose your Professor Bayes would say it too.'

Driving slowly through the bush transfigured in moonlight, I did not feel like adding anything more. My father was looking down at his feet and I heard him mutter, 'The tide of science and reason … But,' he looked back at me. 'But … what tide? The tide of your professor, or the tide of Jim Clark? They are rather different, are they not? And don't tides flow in and out, forming a new and better course sometimes?'

'My tides didn't exactly flow – came more like tsunamis.'

There was a pause. I half expected my father to be preparing a sermon on prodigal sons squandering their spiritual heritage. His eyes turned to the moonfilled wilds we were passing through; but what he said when he looked pensively back at me wasn't what I expected.

'You know, Robert, after our exchange of letters, the thought came to me: all your life I've given you a pretty weak-flowing version of what religion can be. Perhaps I should have encouraged a tsunami or two. The great religious teachers knew all about inner tsunamis; that is what made them great.'

He met my surprised look with steady eyes. 'Robert, it seems that I never got across to you – or for that matter even fully to myself – a fundamental fact. It's this: religious understanding is finally based on *sensing,* experience, not on pig-headed adherence to some fossilized articles of faith, which you think I'm laden with. It's a very old and very universal understanding, but often overlooked – so often overlooked that when it comes, it's likely to come as a tsunami, disturbing: the mind can be opened to a certain overwhelming experience, aye, direct awareness of a divinely powerful force, a transcendent reasoning power – "the infinitely superior spirit that reveals itself," Einstein said of it. "That deeply emotional conviction," he said. Did you know that?'

'Vaguely. You talked of Einstein, but I didn't take it in, then.'

'Well there you are. I didn't give you – or me – enough of the tsunami treatment; scary because one must finally surrender self.'

I did not have time to tell him about Duma's crocodile before he continued, 'I should have encouraged you more into living experience, with that "fierce and practical proximity" that G.K. Chesterton felt about spiritual things. If you must use words, Robert, then speak of encountering that fierce and practical proximity of spiritual power, a living intelligence coursing through all life and matter, the Glory of the Lord – a glory revealed, not just believed in, or inferred, or built up as theory or dogma, but *revealed*, experienced. Robert …'

Now there was urgency in his voice. 'It's so much a matter of *perceiving*. Yes, we all go about our lives in a state of appalling blindness; we exclude so much of the total reality in and around us – so much that it's almost impossible to discuss the matter with someone who's never consciously taken in anything except what his senses have conventionally given him. It's like trying to discuss colour arrangements with someone blind from birth. The workings of nature, its inner constitution, its divineness … to those who are open, it can be *perceived*, not just inferred, uncomprehendingly guessed at. Its proximity is practical and overwhelmingly sensed as we are lost in wonder, love and praise, as Wesley put it in that marvellous hymn.'

'Practical? How can you say it's practical, if it's just a feeling of – wow!?'

'If you can sense the source of all that is right and good, then you will think and act in ways that are right and good; that's practical enough, isn't it?'

Before I could find an answer he added, 'If we're talking about what is practical, in your job here you could speak of recognising divine wisdom in the workings of nature, the great marvel that has yielded these wondrous African wilds, this ...'

Words were beginning to bubble out passionately as an arm waved towards the bush; 'this holy place where the unrestrained workings of nature call on us to respond with care and understanding. Nature does not run on some arbitrary, irrational whim; it is logically ordered. That means, it's explainable in its own terms if we penetrate to that order, as science in its own way tries to do.'

'So, you're saying, we don't need God to explain all that's around us here?'

'I'd say, when we try to explain nature, there's a place for reason of the kind science attempts to grasp; but *how* one perceives that reason in nature is quite another matter, and that is where a deeper, life-changing insight comes in. And it's likely to come as a tsunami, so people find. Sad that your professor has never had that – but then, what'd he do if he *did* have a tsunami? Lose his job?'

He sounded amused, but the remark slipped out of me, 'Well it's no good saying: workings of nature lead to the idea of a god, least of all if you say it's about a loving god – try telling the young hippo that got torn to pieces about a loving god.'

My father subsided. 'If you were to ask what divides your chief ranger and myself, Robert, I think I'd have to say: we divide on this very point, God or no God? The deep underlying unity between logic and the workings of the world, yes, there we agree; the way it all hangs together like a great thought – the way mind transcends it all, the way mathematics works, the fundamental order of our universe that is the very precondition for science; yes we both see that, but then what do we make of it, especially when it disturbs and troubles us? What? Some philosophers say it's simply an illusion, that there's really no order, but try telling that to the practical scientist and technologist whose work arises out of this order. The truth is, we barely have the science, barely have sufficient perception to know clearly *what* to make of it, what makes your chief and me differ. So, our prize-fights as Sibanda calls them tend to go round in circles even though we tread a common ground. But then are we in *no* position to talk sensibly about the existence or not of what might be called God, and whether it matters? The answer has to be: well, what do you directly experience? Do you experience something infinite, the glory of light beyond light, love beyond love? To have that experience gives you a Yes regarding belief. If you don't experience it – then bad luck, I would say.'

While hearing him my driving had become slower and slower; now we came to a halt, as if somehow we were out of ordinary time. 'You know, Dad, I've never heard you speak quite like this before.'

'Well, following that letter I wrote you, one or two tsunamis have swept through me, by God's grace – if you will pardon that expression; understand the word God from John's gospel. To me the correct translation is: "At the beginning was reason, logos. Reason was with God, and God was reason." John also tells us that God is light, the other side to the same coin, reason and light. Nowadays science and reason are supposed to have swept the idea of God away. And this despite the obvious fact that our universe is an orderly creation at its deepest level, what we can see as reason and light. Don't you get puzzled by that orderliness, reason and light sometimes, Robert? Men like Einstein did, but your professor – did he have anything to say about it, that all his science would simply not be possible without nature being the coherent intellectual structure that it is? And was he prepared to account for that?'

I started moving again, driving cautiously past a bulky hippo grazing out in the open. 'I can tell you one thing the prof would say about all this. If this is such a lawful and orderly universe, then all those psychic things – distant seeing, dowsing, even directly sensing the divine – simply can't happen.'

There was no hesitation in my father's reply. 'I'm sure your Jim Clark would say, all those things really *are* lawful at their own level – the level of mind, where mind can truly be seen exerting itself in its own right in the supposedly inert material world. Yes, that independent level of mind, which science is so ridiculously apt to ignore despite the fact that mind, consciousness, is the most direct thing we experience, the very basis for thinking. These mind-based things can and do happen, given the right, lawful conditions, even if your professor is wilfully ignorant of them. And so he falls short of entering the true pilgrimage of our times, of exploring, understanding these mind-based things, the survival of mind beyond bodily death included.'

I heard a firming in his voice. 'That is where we should all be heading, each in our own way, even if an individual's pilgrimage leads beyond what we may happen to like at the moment. So should I be concerned if in your pilgrimage you choose to leave the Church? You have a case: it seems that religious establishments have a special talent for covering real experience under a heap of ritual, comfortable interpretations and dogma, something that can ruin not only true perception, but also right knowledge and right action.'

He nodded, completely sure of what he was saying. 'With that in mind, Robert, we need not ask about the ending to your pilgrimage. One can expect a rough passage at times over the ocean of experience. As T.S. Eliot urged, we should fare forward rather than fare well. But may history not find us, each and all, unable in these times of change to travel wisely with the gift of freedom, to take a harmonious, insightful, constructive course towards fruitful living.'

Fare forward rather than fare well ... the chief had quoted that once, at an exclosure a few days before his leaving. And the idea of exploration, a pilgrimage – how similar, and yet how different seemed the standpoints of the chief and my father! One thing was now becoming clear to me as we neared the camp entrance, the whitened gateposts gleaming faintly in the moonlight: my pilgrimage would be nowhere near complete if I could not find some kind of resolution – perhaps even a transcendence – of their differences. Could such a bridging even throw a link across the gulf to Prof. Bayes? Could my father even join the professor's contempt for 'a snivelling concern for personal immortality'?

I put the question to him.

There was silence. He turned towards the bush spread out in moonlight; its elemental wildness seemed to edge him towards saying, 'Robert, let me strip myself of the easy assurances my trade supplies about a life beyond.' Solemnly he looked back at me. 'This done, I am free to say: your professor shows a greatness of spirit so often lacking in our own timid salvation-mongering.' The tone was now becoming adventurous. 'What good, in truth, is a snivelling concern about some paltry interminable self? Why cling to the limitations of our self-bound expectations? St Paul tells us that God – universal, rational, good – will clothe our inner seed with a body of his own choice, not with the limitations we happen to wrap round ourselves at this moment. So then –' now he was sitting erect in his seat, audacious – 'then why not go forward free of these self-bound limitations, freely go forward to a new creation? Yes, as in Wesley's hymn: "Finish then Thy new creation." Let us trustingly go forward as pilgrims equipped with faith, loving kindness, reason and a clear openness to what is beyond the here and now. Even if your professor lacks a degree of openness, give him credit for seeing that we have the potential, the freedom – and the grace as I would call it – to venture boldly towards a truly brave new world, a new creation. With such a prospect, who should be caught snivelling about their own little self and its fate?'

There was an easy answer to that question. 'Caught snivelling? Me, when I wrote you that letter,' I had to say. 'When things didn't work out the way I expected.'

He subsided with a dissatisfied grunt. 'Then it comes back to what I was saying earlier; that the Mission – God spare us, the whole Church – tends to perform like a comfortable hotel instead of throwing its pilgrims into the storm of living beyond limited self, directly to feel the "fierce and practical proximity" of spiritual things.'

Somewhere, I thought, in all this there must be a rockbottom point of understanding what lay beneath all the fences, the tribes that separated the ideas of my father, of Duma, of Professor Bayes, Sibanda and the plain-spoken Jim Clark. Somewhere ahead was the feel of a resolution, hidden, lying quiet and staring at me like some secret creature; and the final meaning of my story in this reserve was to reach through the wilderness of ideas towards it, the secret creature known but undisclosed, the guarding creature of some new creation.

And now the gateposts; I steered between them, the same two heavy poles through which we had left camp. But, I wondered, were these the same two people returning through them?

'It's been some evening, Dad. The pilgrimage of our times – the term you were using; I hardly expected things to work out like this. But this evening … there's a glimmering of a trail ahead – my bit in the pilgrimage, at least. A new path of putting things together … I'm not even sure how to say it.'

My father began laughing. 'Well then, Robert, the evening has not been wasted on us! You know the saying that the mills of God grind slowly, yet they grind exceeding small?'

'Actually the chief once used it.'

He laughed again. 'Duma? Well, he's one of those who make the mills turn a little faster! Those mills we sometimes tend to dread: the freedom to have experiences, pleasant or unpleasant; the very basis for growth, not fenced conveniently off.'

With Duma's return now close, what experiences lay right ahead? One experience not in view was a prize-fight between the chief and my father; he was due to leave a few days before the chief's homecoming. Next time I was near a fight, though, I was sure a new spectator would be at the ringside – maybe even climbing through the ropes to referee.

The bright lights of camp were now bringing us back to its domain. On this moonlit night we had taken a few steps out of the familiar, garish world, and now there was the task of returning to its affairs. As I drew into the parking area I wondered if there were yet other spheres, spheres which would make a return even to the realm through which we had passed tonight seem like a descent.

Steps upon steps. Would I ever be able to climb them? Would they ever take mankind beyond itself?

PART THREE

Chapter Nineteen

The river winding through the reserve has many sounds, many voices asking endless questions about existence. The rippling of a surface shoal of fish: why life? The hollow roar of floodwater: why death? And from the little hill behind the rest camp I could watch the river disappear in distant haze to question silently on the horizon the very meaning of changelessness and change.

Always changing, yet keeping its identity, the river is as much a paradox as is self. How long does a self exist unchanging? Perhaps only for the moment of a single thought; for the next thought is different and cannot match exactly any that occurred before. The only constant thing is change, a streaming in one direction or another – in any direction save the one we came along. The flow is irreversible, like the river.

And from the hill behind the rest camp, change now shows along the winding road that leads here; a speck trailing clouds of dust which must be Duma's Land Rover back from nine months of change; great change, change which none of us suspected. For with him – so his latest letter told us – would be someone never heard of before, yet already his bride for three weeks. A nurse, he wrote, half Indian, half English, 'a mongrel like myself.' And I was posted there on the hill to warn the camp of their arrival.

It was to be a great event, the moment of their homecoming. A special feast had been prepared in traditional style, with hefty Makanya out in front of the chief's house thundering praise-songs as the chief set foot beside it. And even he, the head game guard, was not going to ask where the meat stewing in all the pots had come from.

Duma looked unsure of himself. Before, he would have dumped his things on the verandah of his house and shot into the bush. Now he was prepared to let time pass, to observe a few social formalities. Yet there was no unsureness about Samantha, his wife. She must have known that all would be watching as Duma opened the Land Rover door to help her out. And she flowed out in one delicate movement, tall and slender, an attractive face set in a generous sweep of dark hair. Perhaps she did not wear the most suitable things for travelling on a hot, dusty day to camp – a frilled, light blouse and boldly patterned skirt; yet they blended into a single announcement coming from every part of her, that we were to have a strong new current of femininity in the camp life. Yes; you could see in her a wonderful complement and compliment to Duma, especially as behind those spontaneously warm gestures was the incisiveness of a very intelligent person.

Everything was set to make the feast a bright success, yet, 'You, Robbie, you're leaving so soon?' Sibanda asked surprised as he saw me going off with the keys of a patrol Land Rover. 'Man, the party's only just getting under way!'

'My notebook ...' I said; and he nodded, his expression turning glum. The whole camp knew about it, a sheer disaster – the notebook packed with the past month's field data on lions was gone, fallen out of a Land Rover bouncing through the bush two days ago. And once more I was off scouring the bush trying to find it until, again, darkness forced me back without the book.

Trudging towards my hut that evening past the chief's place I could see lights on all over the house, and signs of upheaval. Duma spotted me through the window.

'Dammit,' he shouted, 'there's someone holding a whip over *me* now!'

I went round to the front door. From what I could see, the entire house was being rearranged.

'Men simply don't know how to lay things out sensibly,' Samantha remarked as I made my way in among the regiments of dislodged furniture. The ridgeback dogs, ecstatic up to now about the return of their master, seemed to be looking on aghast.

Duma put on a helpless look, a small-boy shrug of shoulders before turning to her, laughing, to topple her gently backwards into an easy chair.

'It's about time you laid *yourself* out sensibly! Hell, you'll be bursting open if you go on like this. And Rob, what about that notebook?'

Now it was my turn to shrug shoulders helplessly.

'I know,' he said. 'It's a sod when that sort of thing happens. Wasn't there anyone in the patrol Rover with you at the time?'

'Yes, I was out with Nsundu. It was he who spotted that my rucksack had opened in the back and was letting everything out.'

'Nsundu? But you can't tell me that a first-rate tracker like him isn't able to find it.'

'We've spent the last two days absolutely combing the route we took. He found my hunting knife – that had fallen out too; but the book … I'd have a lion report ready for you, if it hadn't been for this.'

'And will you go on looking for it?'

'Huh! The termites will be eating it by now, even if it hasn't been trampled to pieces. What's the good of going on looking for it?'

Duma nodded. 'The same sort of thing's happened to me.'

He sat on the arm of the chair beside Samantha. 'Well Rob, there is one last resort, if you care to try it. D'you know a man at Sengwe called Ngoma?'

'Ngoma? But … isn't he the local witch-doctor?'

'If you choose to call him that,' he said coolly. 'He's helped me and other people out of similar trouble. All I can tell you is that he's found lost things before. If you want to call him into the search, then let me know and we can visit him tomorrow.'

'Well, I don't really know if …'

'No need to make plans now. Tell me first thing tomorrow how you feel about it.'

He glanced round at Samantha, flopped out beside him in the chair.

'Well I know how *we* feel about things right now; we'd better start turning in – that's if I can find where the damn bed's got to. Goodnight, Robert,' he said standing up. 'Think about it.'

'Yes, well, we'll see …'

I was so tired that the chief's suggestion was out of my head by the time I reached my hut. It was only next morning, having an early breakfast by myself, that I began working it over.

What a crazy idea!

Still, if you really are to keep to the path of reason Prof. Bayes was talking about, at least you should weigh the pros and cons. Pro: Duma says it's worked before. Let's not worry about *how* it worked, and let's not – for the moment – think that he is simply trying something on. Con: well, it's a very odd way of doing things. If it does work, then why don't you hear more about it?

But the fact remains that if it's worked before, there's at least a statistical justification for trying it again. Isn't that being scientific? Even if going to consult a witch-doctor doesn't seem very scientific.

Yes, I thought, it seems reasonable to try it. In any case I wanted the chief to see the dam that had been built near the northern boundary on the way to Ngoma's place.

So as soon as he was free we set off for Sengwe, leaving Samantha reorganizing the house with the help of Martha.

'It'll be a good thing to get him out of the place while we're busy,' she said.

Duma put on a grimace, sliding a wink towards the beaming Martha as he gave a click with the side of his tongue – a fed up sound in her way of speaking.

'These women!' he groaned in Zulu.

It was an easy journey along the main road, and we talked lions most of the way. Duma had misgivings about the dam. 'The trouble with setting up a permanent water supply is, you concentrate the game. That sandveld community has developed under a shifting population of animals, and fixing it may wreck the place.'

Fortunately when he checked the area he seemed satisfied that the bush was holding its own.

Then on to Sengwe, and the place of Ngoma. There was nothing unusual here, a circle of thatched, mud-walled huts surrounded by trampled earth; a bared, peopled patch beside the road, merging into the goat-stunted bush around it.

Ngoma was squatting outside a hut, busy grinding herbs with an apprentice. Usually there is no mistaking a witch-doctor; you can tell him by the extravagant attire of inflated bladders, strings of beads, animal tails, often seed-pods round the ankles sounding a siss-siss as he walks and dances. All these are props in the spectacular performances of divining and treatment, but Ngoma had very little of this. A few bladders from goats that had been sacrificed hung along with beaded strings on either side of his aged, wizened face. For the rest he was clothed in a mixture of tribal and Western dress, like most people in his area.

'Hau! The One-who-thunders!' He rose eagerly, saluting Duma, but then doubled in a wheezy fit of laughing.

'Ngoma's sense of humour,' Duma observed, 'is something you have to get used to.' In Zulu, 'I see you, Elder,' he said with a hand raised to return the salute, 'But what makes your beer taste so good today?'

Ngoma was pointing at him. 'Look at the mane of the Thundering Lion – a woman now is weaving it into spindly little tassels like warthogs' tails!'

Duma watched him stagger about. He turned to me with a hint of sheepishness. 'The news seems to have got around.'

'What news?'

'You clot. Whoever expected me to come back married? Not even Ngoma, it seems.'

'Perhaps he's finding it even funnier because he did expect it.'

Duma shrugged his shoulders a bit self-consciously. 'Yes, Elder, I have come back with trouble. But also, here there is trouble that is not of my doing.'

And he ushered me forward so that I could tell Ngoma all that had fallen from me.

He listened attentively. 'Hau, that is a heavy loss.' We were asked to sit on the ground outside the hut, and he heard my story again, this time fingering another notebook I had brought with me. He looked sympathetic, no showmanship spoiled the simple humanity and concern at someone's loss.

When I finished he gave a thoughtful grunt, saying he would see what could be done.

The hut behind him had a low entrance, and he half rose to go through it, beckoning us to follow. I hesitated, but Duma was already up, coaxing me inside. And so we entered and sat on the earthen floor to form a circle. The apprentice began singing softly while Ngoma squatted down almost casually, but his look was of preoccupation.

'He finds the singing helps – concentrates the mind,' said Duma. 'If your mind can't do that, then at least keep it open.'

I tried to look as indifferent and scientific as I could, but, 'Of all the things to be doing,' I was saying to myself, 'sitting here, and my notebook coming to pieces somewhere out there in the bush.'

Meanwhile Ngoma had breathed fairly deeply once or twice, and became very still. Was he busy with a crocodile? I wondered.

The grass roof above us damped even the silence as we waited. Of all the things to be doing … Yet as nothing happened in the stillness, perhaps there was a touch of disappointment in the indifferent scientist act I was putting on.

We waited about twelve minutes until Ngoma sighed heavily and stirred himself, abstractedly scratching a leg for a moment before speaking.

He did not look my way but asked me, 'Do you know a pan, a dried-out pan, near the road leading through the reserve to this place?'

'Yes,' I said. 'It's downstream from where I built the dam.'

Ngoma scratched his leg again, still with an abstracted look.

'There are ant-hills just beyond,' he said looking at the ground in front of him, not at me.

'We actually did turn off the road at that place; and we did go over some ant-hills – they jolted the Rover. But we searched there, really thoroughly.'

'And did you look in every hole there?'

'Well, I don't think there *were* any holes.'

'Not even where your ant-bears have been digging up ant nests?'

'I … well I suppose there must have been some ant-bear holes there.'

Ngoma still did not look towards me. 'And you did not search them?'

I felt my facade of superior indifference beginning to collapse. 'Is … is that where it lies, the notebook? In an ant-bear hole?'

And Ngoma looked directly at me for the first time. Perhaps he recognized that only now was I making real, human contact with him.

'You should search there more carefully.'

I didn't know what to do or say. I looked appealingly towards Duma.

Ngoma started to laugh, and rose to go out of the hut. 'Me, I do not expect payment from my friends. Now let us go in the sun. We shall have beer and the One-who-thunders will tell me of all his travels.'

So once again outside the hut I sat as patiently as I could with a bowl of sorghum beer brought by one of Ngoma's wives, while Duma and Ngoma talked.

'Hau! The Fawn grows restless,' said Ngoma after a little time. 'Yes, his book is not safe there; he must go now and collect it.'

As I climbed back into Duma's Land Rover I accepted from Ngoma the invitation to visit him any time I liked. But the acceptance was not very positive. One thing I could not afford to do, I thought, was to get mixed up in a show like this.

We travelled back down the dusty north road in silence. Duma had asked me to drive – not easy with thoughts threshing about like a buffalo-fight. On the one hand I hoped that Ngoma was right, since losing the notebook would be a disaster. On the other hand I hoped he was wrong, because then there would be no raising of a difficult, almost frightening problem of how he did it – and yet, 'You!' another part of me was saying, 'you who think of Bayes as reactionary, who are *you* to cast a stone?'

In the meantime the chief gazed out of his window with an untroubled face, enjoying a fresh look at his beloved reserve. He passed only one remark, 'Ngoma, by the way, was the man who carved that crocodile figure on my desk.'

The comment made me feel uneasy, but I did not say anything.

After what felt a long time we reached the dried-out pan. Of course, I thought, Ngoma could have known about these features all along. I pulled off the road at the spot where the tracks left by the patrol vehicle could still be seen, and we got out among the ant-hills.

After a while of searching I had to give a shout.

'Come and look here!'

Duma hurried across to me. There, in a dug-out ant-hill, half covered by soil, lay the precious notebook. Wondering if it would dissolve in air or turn into a snake, I lifted it out, dusting off soil all over it. It was still readable and I clasped it tightly, not feeling very interested in what Duma muttered: 'I reckon you should've found that book yourself, without having to call in Ngoma.'

I shrugged my shoulders. 'At least I've got my book.'

We returned to the Land Rover without saying anything more and continued towards camp.

I was thinking very hard. Could Ngoma have been in the reserve three days ago, and seen the whole thing happening? The chances of that were fantastically small. Could Nsundu himself have seen the book fall out, and then told Ngoma afterwards to catch the chief in a web of – of what? Not Nsundu, the mentor and good companion in so many journeys through the bush. What motive could there have been? Had Ngoma or anyone else gained anything from this? Not really. Ngoma seemed an open, casual sort of person who had made no show or profit out of this. He had treated the matter as an everyday chore, a small service for a friend. The apprentice seemed casual, too. He had not been sent with us so that he could return praising the powers of his master.

Eventually I asked, 'How d'you think Ngoma did it?'

Duma looked slightly amused, as though he had a private joke.

'He says his mind can become detached, travel at will, and if he wants to find something, he just thinks of it, and there he is, looking at it. But of course, that explanation is absurd, nonsensical, isn't it?'

'Yes, I'd say so.'

'*Why* would you say so?' he asked quickly.

I realized I had been led into a trap, but I was prepared to fight my way out.

I thought for a moment. 'Well, first of all, how's it possible for Ngoma to be in two places at once? We were watching him the whole time, and he has only one body.'

I heard a contemptuous snort. 'And this from a Christian, too!' I tried to cut in, but was not fast enough. 'Ever heard of a chap called St Paul? Didn't he tell the Corinthians about a natural body and a spiritual body? Okay, churchgoers ignore this statement or think it's some kind of allegory; but has it never occurred to you that it might be true, that in some way mind can detach from body?'

'I'm not prepared to take anything like that in the Bible as factual,' I said briskly, thinking back to Chris's arguments. 'It's pre-scientific.'

'Hey?' The chief had not yet caught up with what had changed during his leave. After an astonished look, he began laughing. 'Hell, Rob! Sounds as if someone's been having a go at your religion while I've been away! All right then, don't worry about the Bible. But it strikes me as odd that someone brought up on it should never have thought about a passage like that.'

I shrugged my shoulders. Something here about the conventional fare my father had fretted about, not the fierce and practical proximity of spiritual things. But I wasn't going to say anything. I didn't even meet the candid, assessing glance Duma gave me before he turned to look out of his window to assess instead how the reserve had been faring.

In the end I asked, 'Well, what does Ngoma actually say about all this?'

Furrows down the forehead deepened as he turned in my direction again. 'He says ...' A way of putting it did not seem come easily. 'He says that a person can perceive, can view things beyond physical sight. Remote viewing, some adventurous people in America have called it. God knows; to try to figure it out causes melt-down in the brain. But he does see things that ordinary sight can't see; and this isn't just a story Ngoma has cooked up – it's common knowledge among African tribes.'

'Then why don't books on African customs and magic deal with it?'

He sounded scornful. ‘You should be able to answer that yourself. When nearly every supposedly educated Westerner treats the whole thing with blank disbelief, like you are doing now, d’you think an African is going to press his point? The thing’s too far from present-day scientific preconceptions to look good, and it’s too close to naive occultism to smell right. So d’you think the intellectual Establishment wants to know anything about it? Hah! They jump away from it, just as you are doing now.’

I fell into silence. I had lost count of the number of views on man and his nature that had come bowling past me from different directions here at the reserve. I half expected a flying saucer to land on the road in front of us, and already I pictured little green men with antennae and long, pointed noses jumping out.

‘We’re sorry,’ they say, ‘but we must stop you for a servicing and recharge.’

‘But what do you mean?’ ask the two humans. ‘A servicing and recharge?’

‘Yes, don’t you know?’ The little men look surprised, even a little peeved. ‘You’re our electronic toys, and you need a servicing and recharge every two weeks.’

‘But,’ protest the humans, ‘we’ve been living for *years*, and we’ve never had a servicing and recharge before.’

The little men heap themselves on the road in helpless laughter. ‘That just shows how much you know about your existence!’ they cry. ‘Why, you haven’t been alive two weeks yet.’

‘Where the hell are you taking us?’ Duma asked as I hurriedly had to swing the Rover back to the middle of the road. ‘I’m not ready for a permanent out-of-body trip *just* yet.’

‘You don’t mean to tell me,’ I said sarcastically once we were going straight, ‘that you actually forgot to bring another body along with you, just in case.’

The response was another snort. 'Crickey, Rob, if you could suddenly see all that was really involved – it'd blow your stupid brain. You remind me of your recent visitor, Prof. Bayes. He actually got angry when I talked about this kind of thing – even got annoyed with *me*, as if somehow it's *my* fault that these things happen; some cheeky attempt of mine to undercut what he liked to call "the stable foundations of modern science". For God's sake! All I have to do with it is that I find it happens, and I see no reason for keeping quiet about it. Question the observations and their interpretation; yes, of course. But you're only going to be a scientific fraud if you say that it oughtn't to happen, or that it can't happen because it doesn't make sense or because you know better.'

I could have told Duma all that myself; it was a story begun in his study the day he left, highlighted by Jim Clark. Yet I did not feel like letting him off lightly. Could he talk past Chris and his professor?

'But,' I said, 'Ngoma's story, it actually *can't* happen. Consciousness, the mind, can't just wander off from the brain – think what happens with brain injury, with drugs. Consciousness happens where the brain is.

'Oh?' Duma replied drily. 'Then think of this. If you throw your radio against the wall, what sort of messed-up sound are you going to get from it? But is the sound messed up because the radio waves have been affected? Well, just think of your brain as the radio set. Even if its performance is messed up, how can you say there can't still be a separable radio programme – mind – coming through it?'

I didn't have a quick reply.

He glanced at me as if I were a bit stupid. A moment later he broke into laughter. 'All right, Rob; that was a tough point of yours! I can tell you that I've fought with this kind of thing; there was a time when I found Ngoma's work as way-out as you're finding it now. It gives Bayes's stable foundations of modern science too much of a bloody kick. I've tried to explain these things away really hard – I've tried even harder than Bayes, although you may not believe it. I came clean to grips with the facts – and the facts won. All Bayes has done is run away from the facts, fix the dirty label "occultism" and scamper back to his stable foundations. I asked him to visit Ngoma, and his reply was, I should be ashamed of myself.'

He leant forward, rubbing his chin as if trying to recall something. Then, nodding slightly, he turned to me. 'Perhaps you remember my saying to you, Rob, that if you stopped on the established road and walked a few paces off, you'd find things that the Establishment doesn't even want to believe *exist*. Well, now for once you *have* been off the road. Ngoma's been there all this time, and you've just thought "Oh yes, the local witch-doctor", and laughed. Maybe you still do. Well that's for you to decide. For myself, when I come across facts like that, I want to follow them up – which makes all "good" scientists jump up and down and shout that *I* am not a scientist.'

He paused for a moment.

'Anyway.' His face had become set with a touch of grimness. 'Let's not go any further with that now.'

We were driving into camp. I didn't know quite what to say.

'Well thanks very much for the help – I don't need to tell you how glad I am to have my notebook.'

Duma nodded.

'It seems,' I continued, 'that you can't settle down for long with one set of ideas before something else gets blown along and makes a shambles of what you'd carefully pieced together.'

Duma went on nodding. 'Keep it that way, Robert. Once you erect a fence so that nothing new can be blown your way and create further shambles, then you're *dead*, whether you have one body or fifty.'

Chapter Twenty

'He's one of those who make the mills turn a little faster,' my father had said of Duma. Then what would he have found to say about Samantha? Around her were no mills, but the poise of someone who had come upon the wealth simply of being, and who could share that wealth to the point where self and not-self made little difference. And with the sharing seemed to come a way of knowing, the unimpeded way of knowing I had dimly seen with Jim, with Ngoma; that fusion between a state of being and a state of knowing. In some way she seemed to embody it; yet that could make her seem a menace to those closed off, not free to share in life, to those like Chris.

Some eight days after the Dumas' homecoming, Chris and I passed their house on the way to the office with copies of my completed lion report. Chris said he knew everything about binding manuscripts, so the piles of typing were on their way to the office for this final bit of polish.

We met Duma on his way to the lab, waving back to Samantha as she stood on the verandah, cool-looking in a flowing white dress.

Duma pointed at the sheets of typing. 'I reckon we'll see Robert going about with his notebooks tied round his neck in future. Talk about chucking your records all over the reserve ...'

Samantha laughed. 'You'll have to set up a hot line to Ngoma, Robert, if you go on like that! Chris, what do *you* say?'

'If you want my opinion ...' Chris was on his way along the path to the office. He turned round, a sour look on his face. 'If you want my opinion, there must be someone hot-lining it to

Ngoma already – he got the message about that notebook long before the famous visit. They're crafty, those witch-doctors.'

Samantha leant her head to one side, questioningly, but still with a mild expression. 'Have you ever met Ngoma, Chris, to be so sure of that?'

'That kind of thing ...' A hand wave showed it was too stupid even to finish the sentence. 'Come on, Rob – let's get on with something *real*.'

It seemed he wanted to get away from her assessing look. When I joined him he was irritably pulling out drawers in the office desk, grabbing the stapler to clip the pages together.

He shook the title page at me. 'I'm surprised you didn't dedicate this to Ngoma for services rendered. You're just as much a sucker for this kind of thing, believe as much bull as –' he waved to the Dumas' house – 'those two do.'

I shrugged my shoulders. 'For Pete's sake, let's change the subject. What about that piece of goods you were talking about who came into camp with her parents yesterday?'

'Haa!'

Certainly enough to change the subject. As if performing some kind of displaced mating display he made a show of stacking the typescript, making up one copy for the chief and one for Professor Bayes.

'That piece of goods; the trouble is, she's in hut seventeen, that two-roomed hut – booked in with her parents. Now if only they'd booked a separate hut for her.'

I shouted with laughter, glad to see Chris on home ground once more.

'But small things like that shouldn't worry you,' I said. 'Can't you get her out of hut seventeen on a specially conducted tour?'

'Huh!' He had started driving staples through the piles of script. 'I suppose you'll say I'd better take a few tips from Ngoma about how to drop in for an unobserved visit.' He was starting to look sour again. 'I can tell you one thing. It was bad enough with just the chief going on about this stuff. But with Samantha as well ...'

He kept on muttering all through the final job of fitting strips of tape down the spine to make a backing. Once the tape had been fixed he held up the two copies for final inspection.

'Don't forget to tie a piece of string to the prof's copy,' he said.

'What for?'

'So he can hang it in the loo – that's what he seems to do with most of the stuff given to him for assessment.'

By this time Duma had come into the office with orders for the day, to start a detailed vegetation survey around the northern dam. 'We've got to keep constant check on that area now. If the game concentration starts a dust-bowl round that dam, then – Robert's going to be ploughed in as fertilizer.'

And he asked if Samantha could go with us. She was keen to get to know the reserve from the inside, accompanying staff whenever she felt she was not likely to get in the way. That was no problem for us, especially as she always had something interesting for us in her lunch basket.

'She'll be safe,' said Duma, 'in the stockaded viewing site.' We all knew that outside the stockade, lion and other game made moving about very dangerous.

Three game guards were sent with us to the northern dam; they were look-outs while Chris and I started the census of plants in two-metre-wide strips radiating from the dam. It was hot, scratchy work, trying to take a reasonably straight line through the thorny scrub, and Chris became irritated.

'It's stupid, all this hacking and trampling plants down to make a transect – we're doing more damage to the vegetation than all the bloody game in this reserve put together.'

He became impatient; I noticed he was not looking carefully where he was going. At a point where the transect crossed a narrow game path, 'Huhhh…!' a quick swish of saplings tightened a noose set by poachers, whipping up his foot. He was toppled straight into a thornbush.

He hung there too surprised even to swear, at least until I had broken the saplings to take tension off the noose. By that time the game guards were shouting 'Poachers! They could still be around!' They scattered, looking for footprints as I helped Chris out of the thornbush.

When I got him back on his feet I saw there were no bad scratches, and his boot had saved a deep cut by the wire. But we would need wire cutters to free him.

'Dakwa!' I shouted.

Dakwa had been assigned to guard the survey work.

'I hear you, Great Magic-man.' That was his name for me ever since I had rescued him with Jim Clark.

'Dakwa,' I said in Zulu. 'Help us. Get wire cutters from the patrol car. And see if the wife of One-who-thunders is all right. The stockade will protect her from animals, but not from thieving poachers. Tell her to lock herself in the patrol car till we arrive – and warn any tourists there. They can expect only trouble when human hyaenas are around.'

'Magic-man, I go faster than storm-wind.'

By this time Chris had started groaning about his ankle. It had been twisted as he was thrown by the noose. Yet between all the swearing he muttered, 'At least there isn't an animal hanging from this noose. Those bastards …' and off he went swearing again – partly, I guessed, to cope with the pain.

Dakwa was soon back with wire cutters. Between us we helped Chris hobble to the stockade and lowered him on a wooden bench.

Samantha climbed out of the patrol Rover as we arrived. She had been a nurse, so I imagined she knew what to do. Coming to Chris, she knelt down to hold his sprained ankle loosely between her hands, something I had not expected; yet after a moment it struck me that a healing touch was the very thing one could expect of her. Chris did not react well. A sour look grew on his face as he leant back away from her. What she did seemed to be helping, but he was not looking comfortable about it.

After a while he began fidgeting.

Samantha had a preoccupied look as she took her hands away, saying quietly, 'It wouldn't do to use your ankle too much for the moment.'

Chris moved his foot from side to side. It seemed that his ankle was easier; but some of the discomfort he had felt there now seemed to have moved to his thinking.

'Something must have clicked into place,' he muttered, and stood up. Stepping cautiously, he went to a viewing place in the stockade wall overlooking the dam.

'This stupid dam of yours,' he said turning to me, 'it's too near the boundary. It's a target for poachers. Those bastards are probably out of the reserve already.'

He was right. The game guards came back soon afterwards, saying they had tracked footprints to a hole cut in the boundary fence.

It was late afternoon by this time. Chris moodily looked at his watch saying, 'Well, I've done *my* job for the day. Where the hell's my file of data sheets?'

'You must have dropped it at the snare,' I said. 'I'll get it for you.'

'I'll go.' He began walking cautiously towards the stockade gate. 'There's nothing wrong with my ankle; never was.'

It seemed that he wanted to get away. Samantha was sitting on a log bench watching all this with interest, so I sat beside her as Chris went off escorted by Dakwa.

As he disappeared into the bush I said to Samantha, almost apologetically, 'He's not always like this.'

Her look had followed him, eyes slightly narrowed in her assessing way; yet she seemed intrigued, almost amused. 'What an interesting person,' she said.

I looked at her with a touch of surprise. 'Well at least you can say that.'

Her bland, assessing look now turned towards me. She didn't say anything, but her look seemed to be inviting some comment.

I remarked, 'I think that what you were doing really got under his skin.'

'What did you think I was doing, Robert?' she asked mildly.

'I've heard of healers who do it – holding someone's ankle like that. Chris once said he had an aunt who was a psychic healer or something, and he sounded almost angry about it. People like that shouldn't be around, he said.'

I added, 'As Prof. Bayes's student Wendy said: it's the intolerant, really unscientific side that seems to rub off so easily on people like Chris. Is *that* the kind of training – programming – he got at university? Is *that* what science is made of?'

'Science is made of people, Robert; mostly people who base their security on getting moored, programmed, whatever way you want to put it.'

'That's what the Chief taught me. But what you've just done, how does it work?'

Elegant hands opened outwards to show she really had no words for it. 'The thing works if there's a true need for it to work; that's all I know about it.'

Like Jim Clark had said. I told her about Jim, 'and Chris's reaction about him was just the same.'

Samantha could sense Jim's gloom: 'We are right bang in a dark age,' he had said – the worst ever, because we think we are out of it and call other times dark.

But I felt I didn't need to expand on that. Footsteps announced Chris's return. He was carrying his file of data sheets.

'Let's go,' he said.

We loaded the Land Rover and made our way back to camp. Chris still seemed ruffled, but Samantha had a serene look about her. I had an idea that this irritated him even more. At camp he went off for a shower after unpacking. 'I've been messed up enough for one bloody day. And –' eyes fluttered clownishly – 'the fair nightingale might come out of hut seventeen yet.'

I thought it better not to suggest Ngoma's help again. He needed no accessories once he was smartened up and out bird-watching.

Chapter Twenty One

It was still early in the evening. I sat in my hut reflecting that I had not given the chief his copy of the lion report. A sudden realization – the sheer audacity of ever having tried to write a report on lions – hung about me like a weight holding me where I was, but, 'If it's got this far …' I muttered, and trailed across to the Dumas' house.

'Ah.' At the front door the chief took his copy and stood there already paging through it. 'This is something we really needed, Rob. Come inside for a drink to launch it. And …' He broke off as he saw Makanya hurrying out of the office towards us.

'I see you, Makanya,' Duma called out in Zulu. 'What makes you come bounding here like a cheetah?'

'Sibanda – he has not returned from Sengwe.'

'Not yet? And no radio message?'

He threw out his hands. 'We have empty news.'

'He went to Sengwe for provisions,' Duma said to me. 'Should've been back by nightfall.'

We looked at the sky. The night was clear, and the north road would be dry.

'What could've gone wrong?' I asked.

'Anything. Coming with me to find out?'

I nodded.

'We shall go to search,' Duma said to Makanya.

He turned to Samantha, who had appeared in the doorway. 'Feel like coming?'

She shook her head. 'I think I've had enough for one day.'

He went into his house for a moment, to return with a rifle. Without comment he stowed it behind his Land Rover's seat.

The road was dry and smooth. Even if it meant going all the way to Sengwe, we reckoned we would make contact before long. But as the darkened bush gave way to the village lights of Sengwe, we still had no idea where Sibanda was.

We called at the owner of the largest store. Yes, Sibanda had been there and had gone on to another store. He must have left Sengwe at nightfall.

All we could do after that was go to the police station.

He had been there, of course, for the local news and gossip. Yet where he was now, nobody knew.

The constable on duty seemed annoyed. 'Soon after he left here, Ngoma came. Hau! He was angry, very angry. Foreign people – young, white people – had come to his place, looking for drugs. He wanted us to put them in jail.'

'And then?' Duma asked.

'Our patrol went to Ngoma's place. We were ready to give the foreigners trouble, but they had gone.'

Nothing to make his evening interesting, like rounding people up.

Duma gave the constable a salute. 'Stay well. We shall go to Ngoma's place. Maybe he's told Sibanda of these foreigners.'

Ngoma's place is on the road back to the reserve. Very often there is singing far into the night, but when we arrived there it was very quiet. As we got out of the Rover we could see no sign of life in the circle of huts dimly visible in the starlight.

'What do we do now?' I asked.

'Perhaps Ngoma and Sibanda have got mixed up with the drug people. All we can do is see if any of them have broken into the reserve.'

He was just about to open his door when – 'Hey!' – he let out a frightened yell and leapt back from the cab.

I quickly looked over the front bonnet, to see someone else capering about on Duma's side, almost doubled up and wheezing with laughter.

'Hau!' Some Zulu came from the figure at last. 'The One-who-thunders is not beyond scaring!' It was Ngoma, evidently back on form.

'Well for crying out loud.' Duma leant on the mudguard to watch him as he struggled to control himself.

Some more wheezing and Ngoma levered himself up straight to greet us formally. 'I see you.'

We returned the greeting, mystified.

Now he spoke seriously. 'Me, I am on the look-out here tonight, guarding my place. I tell you this: there is trouble here.' His speech had become energetic, earnest. 'Much trouble. Why do you think my wives and children have been sent early to their huts? There have been white people here, young people, doing trade in stuff that makes our people go mad. They cause trouble; and now they have become *your* trouble, because after I chased them from my place, they headed for your reserve.'

'When was that?' Duma asked.

'Just before your gates close for the night, while Sibanda was in the village gossiping.'

'Did Sibanda come to know this?'

'I stopped his truck on his way to the reserve. He heard it and hurried in. Then I went to the police – catch the foreigners if they came back to me.'

'But we've just come from the reserve, looking for him.'

'You do not know how to look, otherwise you would have found him. But me, I am glad they went to your reserve and did not stay in the village. They know nothing of our ways – they cannot even think that people have ways other than theirs, ways better than theirs. They do not know what correct behaviour even *is*. So that is why I am here, guarding my place against any who might come back.'

He was holding a handful of fighting sticks and a spear; I thought any intruders would do well to keep clear of him.

Duma looked worried. 'We must go quickly to see what has happened, Elder. Stay well.'

'May you find what you look for – and may you learn to look better than you do! Learn to look through darkness; not only the darkness of night, but the darkness of your own eyes. Go well.'

We waved to him and set off on the reserve road at top speed. At the reserve gate we saw the lights of a truck facing us. Duma stopped, jumped out to question the driver.

'*Good* evening,' the driver said tersely, leaning out of the cab window. 'Nice party we're having, isn't it?'

'Sibanda, for God's sake what are you doing here?'

'Doing?' As he climbed out of the cab I could see he was knotted with rage. 'I'm waiting to let the police through the gate, that's what I'm doing. Sent a call for them. I've had enough of the party for one night.'

'What are you talking about?'

'People lying in sleeping-bags all over the place. Just look behind the clump of palms north of Nwede Stream, and you'll see it all there.'

'But …'

'Ngoma – he stopped my truck on the way back, told me about these people heading to the reserve. And when I went in I saw tracks going into the bush north of Nwede Stream – that's what made me find them. And when I asked them if they'd ever heard of reserve regulations, they just told me I was interfering with their freedom – their human rights!'

'How long have they been there?'

Sibanda waved the question aside angrily. 'So I said, "Look, if you go straight out of the reserve, or if you go and book in at the camp, I'll skip laying charges this time. But get right back on the road, now now!" And – and they just talked back. More about their freedom.'

'Stay here, Banda. I'm going straight in,' Duma said. 'One of those stupid tits could get picked up by a lion.'

'Nice freedom it'd be for him if he *did* end like that.'

He was so furious that he almost missed his footing as he climbed back in the truck. 'You'll see their tracks going off the road just this side of the Nwede bridge.'

The fastest ride I ever had with Duma was down to that spot. Normally you do not drive fast in the reserve at night – a collision with a hippo, rhino or elephant can make both parties heavy losers. The chief crouched over the steering wheel, eyes trying to pierce even beyond the range of the main beams. Within a tense fifteen minutes we reached the point where he swung off the road along tracks that headed behind a thick palm clump; in a few seconds we pulled up with three minibuses showing in the headlights.

There was no movement at all, although I could hear a guitar and singing in one bus. We climbed out to walk a few paces to the nearest vehicle. As we got to the cab window, 'All right,' someone drawled from the cab, 'now what's going on here? Trespassing? Poaching?'

The accent was North American, but I could not make out from where. A head with tangled hair and beard showed in the window, chin resting in a cupped palm, and a bland smile on the face.

Duma was very direct. 'Any of you sleeping out in the open?'

'Aw, we're not sleeping. We're making love.'

'Is there anyone out in the open?' Duma repeated.

'I figure we're all in the open. Under God's starry sky. Healthy fresh air – I mean that's what we kinda came here for.'

'Well,' I muttered, 'I can see why Sibanda got nowhere with this lot.'

'Looks like you're worried,' said the face.

'Are you all under cover?' Duma asked. 'That's the first thing I want to know.'

'Seems like you've some good vibes,' the face observed candidly. 'Little agitated, though. We can help with that.'

'I said …'

'Try some meditation, like this.' Palms were pressed together in front of the face, and the eyes closed.

Duma gripped the door handle, but paused as a girl's face appeared behind the other and looked quizzically at us.

'What's with them, Lary?' she asked wearily, one hand stroking a flow of long brown hair off her face. 'Seems like there are more people than animals on this scene.'

Duma gave the door handle a wrench.

'Door's locked,' observed Lary casually, 'so's the lions and things won't get us.'

'That's just as well,' said Duma. 'I'm worried the lions will get stomach ache.'

'Say! A real nature-lover,' Lary exclaimed. 'We sure do appreciate that. Guess there's something kinda lionish about him also, isn't there, Estelle; think his sign is Leo?'

She tossed some more hair behind one shoulder, revealing what was really a very sensitive face.

'No, course he's not,' she said after a moment's deliberate inspection. 'He's Sagittarius.'

'Yeah, guess you're right.' Lary looked Duma up and down. 'Every inch a Saggie.'

'Isn't he just divine?' said Estelle admiringly. 'The real hewn-out-of-granite touch.'

'I want some information out of you,' said Duma. 'People sleeping in the open are in danger of being attacked. Now, are any of your party in the open?'

'How do I know, pal?' drawled Lary. 'This family's free – everybody does as they like.'

'And tell me,' Duma said coolly, 'exactly what you understand by being free.'

'No need to tell anyone – like we just do it. Easier to tell you what's *not* being free,' he said pointedly. 'That happens when somebody interferes.'

'So freedom means absence of restraints?'

'You more or less got the idea.'

'And restraint means absence of freedom,' chimed Estelle.

Duma seemed to be getting intrigued in spite of himself. 'Regardless of anything else?' he asked.

'Like what else?' she said.

'Like harmonizing with what else is around you.'

'Harmonizing? Well, I guess …' It seemed that some facade she had been putting on was not holding too well. 'I guess that harmony is actually what we're aiming for, a kind of going-along with; and …'

She was stopped by a frightful shriek, wild cries first from one then from several others. A whole community suddenly seemed to be in uproar.

'The rifle, Rob, quick,' Duma snapped. 'And flashlights.'

I flung open the Rover, grabbed what was needed and rushed after Duma to where we heard the screaming. Between the buses someone was sitting half out of a sleeping-bag, clutching his face as blood streamed all over him. Three or four young people were running in panic to the buses.

Lary had leapt out of his bus and ran with a torch to where the groaning came from. He peered at the gasping, blood-soaked figure, then swung round as he became horribly sick.

In the meantime Duma and I checked that no animals were close by. 'There've been a couple of hyaenas here,' I shouted, looking at fresh spoor. 'One of them must have taken a bite out of him.'

'Bring round the Rover quick,' Duma ordered. 'We'll get him to the clinic at Sengwe.'

I drove to the victim – he must have been about my age – and we started to help him in.

'Luckily it's a bite in the lower face,' Duma said. 'Eyes are all right.'

'Shall I stay or come with you?'

'You drive. I'll check the bleeding – where's that wadding in the first-aid box?'

I could hear a whine of vehicles in the distance. 'Hear that?' I asked. 'That's Sibanda's party coming along.'

'Don't worry about that,' Duma said tersely. 'We've delayed things long enough already.'

I jumped into the driver's seat and drove as far as the junction with the road; but there Duma made me stop.

'On second thoughts,' he said, 'I think we'd be better at handling what's left back there in the buses. The police can look after this one.'

I parked with lights shining up the road, and a few moments later a police Land Rover pulled up beside us.

'Something for you to take back fast – hyaena attack,' Duma shouted. With a minimum of explanation we had the victim transferred; Duma practically bundled the police back to Sengwe.

Then we went back to his Land Rover and I helped him mop up patches of blood all over the seats.

'What are you going to do about the rest of them?' I asked when we had cleaned what we could.

He started the Rover. 'That,' he said, 'depends largely on *them*.'

As we sided up against the cab where we had our first encounter, Lary was there again, but his face now was a peculiar grey-white, and all he could do was stare at us. Estelle beside him was sobbing, face buried in hands.

'Are you getting out of this reserve,' Duma asked quietly, 'or are you coming with us to camp?'

Lary had clearly had enough. 'We reckon we'll come to your camp,' he said hoarsely.

'Then we'd better move; it's getting late.'

Chapter Twenty Two

Perhaps the police never understood why the chief did not lay charges against the intruders. At least the police had no business of their own to take up with them; they were left to themselves, sitting there all the next day under trees in the camp enclosure, smoking, sometimes talking, seemingly not keen to go out in the bush again after their last night's horror. Yet not only this kept the group in; there seemed a peculiar air of aimlessness about them. New Age travellers, was Chris's immediate diagnosis as we saw them at lunch-time sitting about like run-down clocks, too empty even to be doing nothing. 'And,' Chris added, 'their new age has left them beached in timeless Africa.'

It was well after five when I finally returned to my hut, the day's work finished. I gazed at the second copy of my lion report lying on the table, ready to be posted to Professor Bayes.

Should I send it? I wondered. Was it good enough to send? And if he liked it and raised some sort of scholarship for me to go to his university, should I accept it? What would I gain there, against what I would lose here if I were to be beached out of timeless Africa?

I went to the door of my hut to look out towards the bush, turning over the professor's sermon about taking part in a new creation, and trying not to feel slightly irritated because a bunch of the intruders had collected between my hut and Duma's house. Among them I saw Lary and Estelle. They were all sitting together in a loose circle, not saying much – one girl was quietly strumming a guitar – and smoking. But Estelle, I noticed, had placed herself a little out of the circle. Pensively she was fingering the hem of a long, full skirt that made artistic contrast to the tatty gear of most of the others. She looked away quickly after exchanging glances with me; it seemed she was still feeling embarrassed about the previous night.

I saw that Chris had made his way to a cluster at the other side of the camp, where several girls had collected. One might have expected him to take the opportunity for a performance, and there he stood, talking and parading. Still not sure what to do about the professor's parcel, I took out my hunting knife – the one I had almost lost along with the notebook – and sat on the step of my hut, sharpening the blade on a piece of oilstone.

Duma's voice drew my attention back to Estelle and Lary's group, a few paces away.

'About your bite victim,' Duma was saying as he stood beside the hunched figure of Lary. 'A radio report: confirmation that he's been flown back home to the States for plastic surgery. But not too serious.'

Estelle let her head droop despondently. 'It just seems all so … so impossible – why did they ever do such a crazy thing as sleep in the open? Why didn't you stop them, Lary?'

'Aw, shut up.'

He shivered slightly. It seemed he still hadn't got over the shock.

'We really didn't want to make trouble,' Estelle murmured to no-one in particular, bunching herself and looking wide-eyed into the ground. 'It all seemed so natural, just to pull off the road and – and, well, strike up something with Mother Africa.'

Duma smiled grimly. 'Africa is a funny sort of mother to have,' he remarked, 'with a houseful of hyaenas.'

She turned her head, looking up at him thoughtfully. But no-one said anything, so Duma turned to go.

'Are you stocked with food for the evening?' he asked.

'Oh yeah, thanks,' said Lary. 'Yeah, plenty.'

'Well, if you're fixed up, then I'm going to my house.'

More silence, and the chief started to walk away. Estelle looked up at him again as though something was on her mind, but the look faltered and she turned back to fingering the hem of her skirt, head pensively to one side.

There was no more talking. To the side of Estelle the blonde guitarist was cradling the instrument in her lap, too dispirited to do more than pick a few chords. I realized that the scraping of my knife over the oilstone could have been irritating, and as I glanced across to the group again I saw that Estelle now was hunched with head resting sideways on her knees, hair streaming over her skirt. She was gazing at me.

Self-consciously, I tried making less noise sharpening the knife, and she lifted her head.

'Guess you'd like to cut our throats with that thing,' she called to me.

Lary glanced up at her, then at me. His mouth became pulled to one side in a sneer before he lit another cigarette and went on staring vacantly into the ground in front of him.

I replied, 'Worse things happen in this game reserve than last night's scene.' A thought came to me that the three Graces' performance was much more interesting.

She rose to stretch herself as if trying to ease off something that she felt confining. Then with the question, 'What d'you use that knife for?' she came across to me.

'This knife? Oh, it's useful sometimes, prying open bark to see what's killing a tree, collecting specimens from a dead animal – some rangers have even had to use a knife in defence against a poacher or a lion.'

'Is this where you live?' she asked as she came nearer the hut door.

'It's where I sleep – when I have time for it. I live out there,' indicating 'there' with a nod towards the bush.

'You're so lucky,' she said quietly.

'That's just what's worrying me. I might have a chance to go to university.'

'You'd be crazy to go. Absolutely crazy.'

She sat down beside me on the step at the hut entrance, head cupped in her hands, staring towards the bush.

'I went there.' Her soft voice sounded lifeless. 'Lasted there a year and then freaked out. The whole set-up seemed plain idiotic.'

'In what way?'

'I don't know. Maybe it was just the courses I chose. I wanted to find out about myself, so I took things like psychology and biology … oh gee – if you really want to find out about yourself, really go deep into your consciousness, then don't take psychology. All they dished up was a whole lot of theories and hypotheses – as if that's all we could ever be, just a tatty junk-heap of hypotheses and parameters, and not real people at all. I almost wanted to drug the prof's coffee – he sure would've seen some parameters then!'

She drew up her shoulders and giggled, coming a bit more to life.

'You know,' I said, 'that might be all the more reason for going to university – to, to show that there is more to people and to life than just a lot of abstractions.'

Her gaze was still out towards the bush. 'And d'you think they'd listen to you?'

'I don't know. But are all the professors like that?'

'Maybe not. I've heard of other places, faculties where there are some fantastic people. Maybe I just wasn't lucky. All I can say is that if I'd come across more *real* people, then I wouldn't have freaked out.'

Prof. Bayes's urging came back to me: 'It might sound funny, but to me that's almost a reason for freaking in.'

She turned to look at me in her frank, open way again. But she didn't say anything until, after a pause, head cupped once more in her hands she looked out towards the bush murmuring, 'It's so wonderful just to be here.'

'How long d'you think you'll be staying?'

'Depends … depends on the others.' She looked sideways – perhaps a shade disdainfully – towards the group she had left. Then her head turned round to look behind her through the open door into my hut.

'Where d'you eat?' she asked.

'Kind of canteen with the other rangers.'

She glanced across at Chris, picked out now by one of the camp floodlights. He was still performing.

'Is that one of them there?'

'Yes.'

'He looks a real creep,' she said.

I laughed. 'He's not all that bad. But he got a bit stuck on hypotheses and parameters while he was at university.'

'And …' Her look as she sat there beside me on the hut step was intent. 'Is that really what you want? Get stuck too?'

'I want to, to get totally unstuck, to break free of things like hypotheses, guesses; I want to be able really to *know*.' I thought of Samantha, Jim, Ngoma: somehow they could tune in directly. 'I don't know how to put it, but some people – they can reach a state of consciousness, reach a state of being where they can enter a state of knowing, a state where they simply *see;* a state where they can dump hypotheses, speculation, and come directly to insight.'

'Gee!' She looked at me partly amused, partly puzzled, perhaps also partly understanding. 'People in the ivory towers say: you just can't *do* that! D'you *really* think that's possible?'

'Intuition, sensing, whatever words there are for it: some people seem good at it.'

Once more there was the frank, open look; but deepened, now. 'Guess that places like colleges won't get you anywhere with that. All the same …' She placed a hand lightly on my shoulder. 'I wish you luck when you get there. Honest, I wish you luck.'

'If I need any luck,' I said as I pressed her hand, 'I'll use the luck you've just wished me.'

We looked at each other for a moment that did not seem measured by ordinary time. A silence, a stillness had opened out that needed no disturbance. But one part of me would not dissolve into this state of openness, this emptiness-and-fullness. I started asking, 'What did you do after you dropped your courses?'

Her face turned a bit diffidently back towards the bush.

'Oh, I drifted around, doing a lot of stupid things, I guess. But through it all I managed to finish a secretarial course. All the time I was wanting to find out about myself; *know* something of what I'm all about. And I couldn't find any good place to start looking. Then this collection of us –' a wave towards the group – 'from Canada, from the States, got together, decided to make the African scene, and …' she gave me a slightly ironic nudge with her shoulder; 'well, for better or for worse, here we are!'

'Still looking for what you are?'

A more sombre tone. 'I guess so.'

'It seems a long way to go looking – roam all the way here, when the place where you'll find most about yourself is right inside.'

I felt her shoulders shrug a little. 'I know. Everybody said that. But that doesn't stop people like us from wanting to go to the ends of the earth, all the same. I guess –' she cast another glance at the group she had left – 'I guess a lot of us will end just nowhere, wherever we go. But from the churches to the colleges to the guru freaks, you go from one phoney thing to the next, until … a hyaena bite tells you where you've been all along.'

The group was now beginning to stir. We could hear some talk of supper.

Lary, still sitting bunched on the ground, started to look round for Estelle. His face opened in disbelief as he saw us sitting side by side on my hut step.

'Estelle,' he called sharply, 'let's go eat.'

'I don't want anything,' she called back. 'I'm staying here awhile.'

Slowly he rose, deliberately, as threateningly as he could, before lumbering across to stand with hands on hips surveying each of us in turn.

'Come,' he said to her after a pause.

'I don't want to.'

'I said, come.'

He thrust out a hand to pull her up.

'What,' I asked, 'were you saying about freedom last night? I thought you said that everyone in your party could do as they liked.'

With a heavy turn he faced me, a look of threat shaping his expression. Then almost lurchingly he moved towards me, held in an animal programme that read out destruction. I must have involuntarily tightened my grip on the knife; he looked down at it for a moment, too furious to say anything coherent, then backed away a little.

Estelle slowly rose, a sad tinge of disgust unsteadying her voice: 'Oh, gee, I don't want a scene.' One hand passed dejectedly across her forehead as she took a few erratic paces alongside the hut wall before stopping to survey us.

'Okay,' she murmured, drooping slightly. 'Let's go and eat.'

Slowly she trailed away after the others, with Lary bristling behind her.

So much for freedom, I thought.

Chapter Twenty Three

An hour later I had to be out on patrol again.

'Could I ask one of the new crowd to go with me?' I would have liked to ask the chief. 'Show her more of what the bush is really like?'

But there are standing orders about game reserve staff not intruding into the affairs of visitors. The incident on my doorstep could have been challenged as an intrusion. In any case, it would have been impossible to take anyone out that night. The fence near the northern dam had again been cut by poachers, and a bullet loaded for rhino horn could take anything as its target. I would have to wait till the next day before I could hope to see any more of Estelle.

About midmorning I passed the laundry unit on my way to the garage to take out a patrol Rover. Standing beside a laundry table was Estelle, collecting some clean washing. With her was the guitar-playing blonde who sat beside her the previous evening.

'Hi,' Estelle said.

'Hello. Not going out today?'

'They've all gone except Gail and me. We stayed behind to try to get things cleaned a little.'

'Then will you be going out after lunch, this afternoon?'

She shrugged her shoulders and half sat on the laundry table. 'Will you be taking a party out this afternoon?'

'No. I've got to check some fencing – a daylight check before going out tonight to look for poachers.'

'Tonight? You mean you go out at night, into all this wilderness?'

'Night is when a lot of the action is. At the moment a gang is trying to poach rhinos for their horn – smuggling the stuff to Asia.'

She paused, giving me her frank look.

'It must be real adventurous, your kind of life.'

I gave her a doubting glance. 'You know, that is actually the part that becomes the most boring, the cops-and-poachers scene. As far as I can see, it discovers nothing, it resolves nothing.'

She seemed faintly puzzled. 'Guess it's the kind of thing people make movies out of, turn into novels.'

'To me that's just a distraction from what a game reserve really is all about. Even a distraction from what life is finally all about. I wish … you know, I hope you stay here long enough to … well, to let me show you a bit of what I think *really* matters in a place like this.'

There was the frank, open look again. 'I'd love that.'

Eyes were lowered towards the ground in front of her as she murmured, 'Guess I've learnt a lot here already; things I didn't expect to learn about, perhaps didn't even want to learn about.' She looked a little troubled, half sitting on the edge of the table, one leg swinging uneasily. 'It's not turned out how I expected at all.'

I nodded. 'Well, that makes two of us. You know, the very first day I was here the camp superintendent said to me: there's something about the bush that starts making you ask questions, scary questions …'

I broke off. 'Anyway, I'd better not start on this, otherwise I'll never get round to what I'm supposed to be doing before lunch, and the chief ranger – that's John Duma – will have me skinned.'

'What are you supposed to be doing right now?'

‘Well, as it happens, I’ve got to check that no rubbish or anything was left where your buses were parked the night before last.’

‘Oh.’

Her eyes were again lowered unsteadily towards the ground.

But within me I could feel something rising like a hot dart. ‘Would … would you like to come with me?’

The eyes were raised, becoming rounded. ‘Right now? Are you – I mean, is that allowed?’

I laughed a bit unsurely. ‘You and Gail could always come as official observers – to check that I don’t hijack any valuables’

Gail half turned her head away. ‘I don’t want to go anywhere near that place again, after what happened.’

She looked back at Estelle. ‘But, Stelle, why don’t *you* go? I can handle the laundry.’

Estelle’s eyes were dancing undecidedly. ‘Gee, what would I say to Lary when he comes back?’

Gail replied drily, ‘Say it’s the official observer thing.’

Estelle ran her fingers down a fall of hair at the side of her face. She looked even prettier with the touch of agitation playing about her.

‘Will you be long?’ she asked.

‘Back before lunch, easily.’

So I had a passenger in the cab beside me as I headed up the north road for the Nwede stream.

It was close to noon, and the sun was directly above us, beating down on everything that could not escape to the inky patches dropped beneath the denser bushes and trees.

‘Gee, it’s so hot,’ Estelle said. ‘How ever d’you survive here?’

‘Doubt if I could survive anywhere else. I’ve thrived on this heat all my life.’

'All your life? You mean, you've been around here always?'

I nodded. 'On a mission only ninety k's from here. That is, except for the times when I was sent away to boarding school, and hated it.'

'You lived on a mission?' The question was half an exclamation, as if the idea seemed exotic.

'Yes. My father is a missionary.'

That didn't seem so romantic. 'So you must be very religious,' she said a trifle distantly.

'You know, Estelle, it might sound funny, but ...' I glanced towards her. She was looking at the road ahead; her expression seemed cool. 'You know, so many things got turned upside down when I left the mission to work here, that now – well, now I'm not even sure what "being religious" actually means. What do *you* think being religious means?'

She half turned to me.

'Being religious?' she said casually. 'Guess it's when you believe a whole lot of things – even when you know it's nonsense to believe them. But you go along with it because ... well, it comes down to giving you a boost. Guess it makes you feel you belong to something that'll see you right in the end.'

'No!' A kind of explosion made me bang the steering wheel with my hand, and she turned to look at me, surprised. 'No! That's – okay, that's something like I used to think too; a self-preserving kind of club that gets hold of you with the idea of doing something for you. But Estelle – there is something *else;* I saw it when my father came here last, when I told him I had pulled out of religion. Then we found we were talking to each other in ... in a new kind of way. There was something, something beautiful, a kind of spirituality, delicate, which was there between us once we'd pushed the beliefs, doctrines, dogma and stuff to one side. And just glimmering there on the horizon, something was there that made me think, “Why, that is the direction towards *real* religion; that is what real religion is about.” Sounds crazy, but it was only after I thought I’d stopped being religious that an idea of real religion actually began dawning on me!’

She was looking at me in her frank way again. ‘And the old man back on the mission, how does he take it all?’

‘It was tough, of course, when I left the mission for the job here. But … well, we seem to understand each other so much better since that happened. His last visit here was perhaps the best time we’ve ever had together.’

‘He sounds a great guy.’

I took up her way of speaking: ‘He sure is.’

She smiled at me, very sweetly. ‘I’d love to meet him,’ she said.

Then a serious, worried look came over her as she turned to gaze ahead. I was starting to slow down for the small Nwede bridge.

‘So here it is,’ she murmured.

Yes, there were the track marks going off the road towards the low clump of palms. I drove along the tracks and in a few moments we were at the patch of grass that had been almost flattened by vehicles and people.

‘What a mess,’ she said quietly.

I opened my door. ‘Well, it could be worse. Would you like to get out?’

She nodded. ‘If it’s safe.’

‘It’d be safer if you stayed inside, but let me case the joint first. Then, come out if you’d like to.’

I climbed onto the cab roof and scanned the area carefully. Elephant come here quite often among the palm thickets, but there was no sign of them, nor of any other big game. Taking my rifle out of the cab, I came round to her door and opened it.

'It's all kinda exciting,' she said as she climbed out. 'But gee, what a load of idiots we were the night before last, just getting out all over the place like that.'

'Oh well, one lives and learns here – or if you don't learn, you stop living pretty quickly.'

'Yeah,' she said quietly, and took my hand with the trustingness of a girl. As she looked at me a superbly luxuriant smile came. 'It's just great, here.'

She swung my hand backwards and forwards as if discovering newness, freshness in life. Then both her arms were flung outstretched above her head, letting my hand fly away as she did so.

'Oh, I feel so free here,' she cried up to the sky and the sun above her.

She stood with hands reaching up like some priestess for a few moments, before gently lowering her arms and saying, 'It's so great, to get out of that jeep and just be able to stand on the ground, with the bushes and everything here all around you; feel the air and hear the stillness mixed with all the sounds everywhere.'

She glanced about her at the dense stream-side bush and palm clumps. 'Maybe we weren't such idiots to camp out here after all. It looks safe enough.'

I gave a short laugh. 'That's just the trouble! Meanwhile, there could be a lioness behind that palm clump over there, sizing you up for dinner.'

'Not to mention the hyaenas,' she murmured looking at the patch of trampled grass she was standing on, the site of the disastrous camping spree. 'Mother Africa – gee, as your chief was saying last night, she sure is a funny kind of mother to have.'

She stood silently absorbed in her thoughts. After a few moments I started the job I was supposed to be doing, checking the site for anything left there. I had zigzagged over about half the area when she called to me.

'Can I help you?'

'No thanks. Actually, almost nothing's been left – just these few bits of wrapping. You know, it's amazing what one can reconstruct simply by looking at the grass and sand here: where the buses were parked; where the Land Rover went; where the – well …'

She came up to me. 'Where Matt was … where he was attacked?'

'Yes.' I pointed out the area. 'Hyaena spoor trodden over by shoeprints. Grass flattened by a sleeping bag. It seems one or two jackals have come since then, attracted by blood left on the grass.'

She turned her head away. 'Oh, how horrible.' Her whole body swung round and she covered her face with her hands.

And as she stood there, slightly stooped and alone, it seemed wrong to deprive her of feeling all that was passing through her. I made no movement until she lifted her face again and gave her head a little shake. I came up to her and put a hand round her waist.

'Would you like to get back inside the Rover?'

She leaned against me for a moment before saying, 'No, I'll stay here while you finish searching the place.'

And there she remained standing, meditatively, near the blood-stained grass that was now covered in ants. She made almost no movement until I had nearly finished combing the area. Then she turned round to come slowly across to me. She did not say anything; she simply watched. And I knew from her silence that something of our surroundings had sunk in. It was the silence that tends to grow when people are in tune with each other and with the bush; something you hope will be felt after leaving the cities, the towns, the rest camps, and come to a place where the world ends and has its beginning.

In fact we said very little until we arrived back at camp.

The others had not yet returned. Gail was there at one of the small kitchen units, getting some lunch together. With a silent look rather than a 'goodbye' Estelle left me at the garage, gliding off to join Gail.

The two of them were still at the little kitchen when I walked past from the garage on my way to get my own lunch. The buses had come in by then, and as I passed the kitchen I heard the cutting sound of Lary's voice to one side of me.

'Well, just look who's here.'

His expression made it obvious that 'here' was the last place he wanted to see me.

'Hello,' I said, trying to sound matter-of-fact as he came up to me. 'Had a good outing this morning?'

'Guess all that matters is, we're all going out this afternoon.' He turned meaningfully towards Estelle. '*All* of us. So –' a sideways look at me – 'let's get on with our own affairs, shall we?'

And after lunch, when I was about to go to check the fence near Mkomo, I saw the three minibuses rumbling out through the camp gates towards the heat-sapped bush.

Chapter Twenty Four

Daylight was fading by the time I returned to camp, pulling up outside the chief's house to report back. Near the house was the group that had collected yesterday evening, six sitting together in a loose circle – but this time at the further side of the house from my hut. Had Lary herded them off deliberately? I wondered. Little puffs of cooler air gave an unsettled feeling; Estelle was sitting bunched in the shivery feel of dusk, hands round her ankles, positioning herself again just slightly outside the rough circle made by the others. Lary sat to one side of her, Gail to the other, once more with her guitar.

Duma was standing there; they were discussing the hyaena attack.

'Well, maybe ...' Estelle was murmuring, 'maybe it could have been even worse – damaged eyes, bite through to his brain.'

Duma's response to Estelle's remark was a little caustic: 'Maybe not worse as long as there aren't any legal proceedings. Anyway, if there's nothing more you need from me then I'm going off to supper.'

'No, no we're fine,' Lary said, getting to his feet as if to trail to their huts. But Estelle remained where she was, making no movement at all.

'C'mon. What're you waiting for?' Lary asked.

'I don't want to go yet.'

I was still standing beside the patrol Rover, and Lary swung an unwelcoming look across at me.

'Let's go eat,' he said turning back to her.

She did not move. The rest were still sitting, doing nothing in particular. Gail fingered her guitar uneasily. 'It's still early to eat,' she said, sensing that Estelle needed some kind of back-up. But even as she said it she gave a little shiver. It was becoming dark, and a feeling of unprotectedness, of inner chill seemed to have touched her.

'It's all been the last thing we reckoned on, the thing with Matt,' she said listlessly.

Duma nodded solemnly. 'Mother Africa doesn't let you reckon on very much.'

Estelle kept looking into the ground. 'Just what's been going through my mind all day. The things we were saying last night … Mother Africa. I guess I don't even know why I used those words, "Mother Africa". And …'

She looked up at Duma. 'And then, you were saying that Africa is a funny sort of mother to have. I don't know, but …' She stared back at the ground again. 'There's something deep, something huge, silent, mysterious about the whole thing …'

That 'something about the bush – its openness, its hugeness,' which Sibanda had once spoken of so fatefully.

'Aw, c'mon,' Lary said impatiently. 'What's there to figure out in a dump like this?'

Duma turned inquiringly to him as though the question had a sizeable answer.

Gail thoughtfully plucked a string of her guitar. 'I guess Mother Africa is a natural enough name to think of. All we've been seeing here – that incredible creativity just everywhere. Don't the words Mother Africa symbolize all that creativity?'

She looked up at Duma to see if he agreed.

He nodded. 'A creativity that among other things seems to have shaped our own physical bodies and the needs, wants, desires that go along with a body. But – this is where Africa becomes an odd sort of mother to have: your own individual needs and desires, your own personal hopes and expectations, your plans and defences – they don't seem to matter all that much to her. Everything can go horribly wrong in a hailstorm or the bite of a hyaena. What does that suggest to you?'

Estelle made a try, saying slowly, 'I guess the bush really brings it home to you … your impermanence. And yet, it's so strange; in a city, when that kind of thing scares you, you just close in on yourself, try to fool yourself, get high on some trash. But here, there's a feeling that you should be kind of open to it all, be ready to sense it; somehow you open out to the whole set-up in a queer kind of acceptance. It's telling you something, something … pure, silent, secret.'

Some secret that Cheryl must have read. Duma eyed her steadily for a moment. 'What,' he asked her, 'what secret is it telling you?'

'Well,' she ventured, delicately picking her way among words, 'it's telling us where we have been, what's made us, our past evolution. That's deep, huge, but from there you can also see where we need to go, our next step in evolution. Here it's laid out before you like nowhere else, like …'

She turned towards me, as if she wanted to say, 'like that deepening when we checked the camping place.' But a glance at Lary, still standing to one side, hands in pockets, made her falter.

'Time to go,' he was saying.

That seemed to make her want to stay. 'It all reminds me of something I came across at college,' she murmured. 'Guy called Thomas Huxley; wrote that human progress means reaching beyond what goes on in the wilds, changing survival of the fittest into making things fit for survival of people; the great work of helping one another, he said. That's *so* big, seeing he studied animals all his life and then at the end of it said, get your act beyond animal living.'

My thinking reeled back to Prof. Bayes; this was the core of his idealism, the root of his new creation. I was about to say so but Duma's response was quick: 'That *is* very big. Huxley's *Evolution and Ethics*, still hardly grasped even though written over a hundred years ago. Taking part in a new creation that we have the potential for; getting beyond self-interest to the next stage in evolution while still learning what we can from this stage. And here – ' he gestured towards the bush – 'is the cradle of it all.'

Something seemed to be settling in Estelle's mind. I watched her rise in a single, graceful sweep, easing herself out in a wide-armed stretch as though feeling released. Then tossing her long brown hair loosely over her shoulders she said, 'That's so right. Here in these wilds, all this seems a little more clear and real. It's a bit more … more direct and pure. And more drastic also.'

Duma raised his eyebrows, impressed, and nodded.

'That's one reason,' he said, 'why we try to keep this place from being turned into a tip.'

I saw her walk a little distance from the group to stop close to the Land Rover I leant against. There was a touch of indecision in the way she stood. Lary was still slouching with hands in pockets, but his lowered head looked threatening. 'It's time to go eat,' he called to her.

Gail also stood up, followed by the others; but Estelle took no notice of them.

'Are you going out on patrol again tonight?' she asked me.

'Yes. As soon as I've had time to bolt down some supper.'

She put a hand on the patrol Rover.

'Wish I could go too,' she said quietly.

Then a glance towards Gail who was giving her an uneasy look seemed to bring her back to the group. She shook herself, and with a murmured 'Oh, well,' slowly began moving back to them.

'Take care of yourself,' she said looking over her shoulder towards me.

'Take care of *your* self too,' I replied with a glance across to Lary.

'C'mon,' Lary was calling angrily.

She paused a moment, half turning to me. 'Guess I've a lot to take care of, and a lot to sort out.'

As she passed Duma I heard her ask, 'D'you think it's possible for me to come visit you, later this evening?'

Chapter Twenty Five

Next morning was time off for me; time to catch some sleep after a night of futile patrolling and one more murdered rhino. I was in my hut paging uncertainly through the lion report to be sent to Professor Bayes when I heard a knock on the door. Gail was there, breathless and holding a note up to me.

'It's from Estelle,' she said between panting. 'There was such an almighty row last night – Lary performing again – and ...'

She pressed the note into my hand. 'We're leaving right away, all of us.'

The folded bit of paper felt like lead in my hand. I looked at her, stunned, waiting till she recovered more breath.

'Phewhh.' She swept some hair away from her face. 'Estelle wanted to come across to you to say goodbye. But Lary – he threw another tantrum, so she asked me to give you this, fast.'

I felt her press my hand again as it limply held the note. 'Oh, gee, Robert.' Among the urgency was the fresh look of honesty in her face. 'It's all been such a crazy mess, our visit here, but ...' She let my hand drop as she turned to go, 'maybe things will come right, later. I do hope so, honest I do.'

She hurried off, leaving me emptily unfolding the piece of paper. It had been written almost in a scribble.

'Dear Robert, Please – there's a forwarding address on the back – please write to tell me what's going to happen to you. Are you really going to college, which one, when? I'll write soon. I'm leaving with the others because it would be terrible for us all if we had a complete bust-up right now. Please do try to understand. This is going to end, I swear it, and I'm positive we'll meet again – soon. I do *so* want to come back, when I'm ready for it.

'Love – and do, please, keep in touch with me. Estelle.'

Rush round to see her – that straight away flew into my head. But quickly I realized it would help nobody if I did. Then send her a note? 'Yes, I'll be writing to you, today. Come back soon.' But if she'd decided to avoid 'a bust-up right now' by leaving in this way … heavily I sat down at my desk and tucked her note in a drawer, realizing that I had to honour her decision by showing restraint too, and not risk another scene.

I wandered round to the office, not quite sure where to go, what to do with myself. From the office door I saw the three buses on their way out, rumbling along the main drive-way. There, framed in the window of the first cab, I could see Estelle. Not knowing what else to signal, I gave her a very deliberate thumbs-up sign. She responded by waving, also deliberately; and with the dust of the buses still in the air I went straight to my hut to parcel up my lion report for Professor Bayes.

Then a letter, a morning letter to Estelle. It was long, yet it felt light in my hand as I carried it together with the parcelled lion report to the office where the mail bag lay waiting.

Sibanda was sitting behind the office desk.

'Just put another letter in the mail bag, will you, Robbie,' he said tersely.

'To whom?'

'To your father's Great Father, asking that we don't have any more like the collection we've just got rid of.'

I laughed. 'Perhaps the Almighty has taken to sending them here for their improvement.'

He spoke even more tersely. 'In that case, add in your letter that we could do with some extra staff and equipment down here. An angel and a flaming sword, like what was set up outside the Garden of Eden when Adam and Eve were kicked out. That would come in handy.'

I left the office murmuring, 'Could be there's an angel among that "collection" already.' But I knew as simply as I could breathe that neither she nor I could allow ourselves to get stuck where we happened at this time to find ourselves.

From then onwards the mail bag – a zebra-skin sack with a heavy flap to keep out the rain – became a kind of extra-galactic presence. In it would, or perhaps would not, be news formed in realms beyond any placing of my hopes, my imaginings, as days passed without a quick response from Estelle, or from the university.

A week after Estelle's leaving, a first materialization took place: a post card from her. It seemed written under stress. Please, just think of her. It seemed that the letter I wrote on the day of her leaving had not caught up with her.

A second materialization happened in the mail bag while I was busy loading a Land Rover for survey work. Chris brought a letter round to me, sauntering up with the remark that I'd better open it away from the petrol drum. 'It's from the prof. If I know anything about his letters, they just aren't safe.'

I held up my messy hands. 'Maybe there's a form or something I have to return.'

'And you don't want to sully the fair image of the university with grubby fingers? Want me to open it?'

Anxiously I nodded.

'Well, I don't like doing this to a friend,' he said gravely. Holding the letter at arm's length as though it might explode, he opened it cautiously before sitting down on the front bumper to read it, pompously taking off the professor.

I soon dropped my work, and Chris, reading faster, dropped the mannerisms.

'"... Since receiving your report, I have taken the liberty of making some enquiries on your behalf about funding. On the strength of your work I have been able to secure you something that, all going well, will carry you through to a research degree. If you would like to make formal application for university entrance, then let me know promptly, and I shall speed things up from my end. The new academic year starts in two months' time, so if you wish to enrol as a student of this university …" Hey! Let me be the first to congratulate you!'

I stood gazing into the Rover, speechlessly.

'C'mon wake up!' Chris shouted. 'Let's go and tell the chief!'

We hurried to the office. Duma and Makanya were briefing Dakwa and other game guards there. I could not say anything, my feelings could not be sorted out. Amazed, awed, even saddened by the thought of leaving here, I blankly handed Duma the letter.

What would he have to say to the idea of my leaving?

He took one glance at the letter and grinned. 'So he's let you know, has he? Well, I can tell you now that quite a lot's been going on behind the scenes. Congratulations, Rob.' I found a hand being thrust out to shake mine. 'I think you've deserved it.'

'But, but what if I don't want to leave here?'

Duma leant against the office counter, his arms folded.

'How many years of active life d'you reckon you've got ahead of you?'

I still looked blank.

'Let's say more than forty. At the end of it you'll think yourself pretty wet if you didn't take time off now, so's to make the remaining years a lot more effective.'

All I could do was scratch my head.

He broke into laughter. 'All right, Rob! You won't be losing contact with the reserve. You can come back every vac. if you want to – I've fixed that up with head office already. Your lions will just have to get along without you now and then!'

Makanya preferred to make a comment in his own language. 'It is time the Fawn-who-walks-with-lions became the Buck-who-walks-with-baboons, showing city people what can be learnt here.'

Dakwa looked thoughtful. 'Me, I say the Magic-man must take a strong animal spirit with him to do that.'

I had told him of the secret creature of the moonlit night with my father. But now thoughts and feelings swirled. I could not say anything. How I had always wanted to go to a university! But could I satisfy all that Prof. Bayes would expect from me? And it would mean having to leave the reserve. Could I live anywhere else?

'Come on, Robert, snap out of it,' Duma said briskly. 'I'm waiting for that Rover to check the exclosures. Bring it now now now!'

And after that the pressure never let up all day. The rush from one exclosure to another pushed the letter out of my mind. That evening, sitting at the desk in my hut, the letter came back to my mind with a feeling of not-belonging, of emptiness. Estelle's conversation with me on the hut step drifted through my thinking. 'You'd be crazy to go. Absolutely crazy,' was her first reaction.

And mine too. But we had also talked about freaking in to a university.

'It is time …' Makanya's words gnawed at one corner of my mind, 'It is time the Fawn-who-walks-with-lions became the Buck-who-walks-with-baboons, showing city people what can be learnt here.' Something, in a way, that Prof. Bayes had said. 'Who could decline a role in this new creation?' he had asked. And, fare forward rather than fare well – a charge voiced both by the chief and my father. 'I wish you luck when you get there,' Estelle had said. And here in the professor's letter was there not more than a little luck?

Chapter Twenty Six

The next morning then, I put a letter addressed to the university in the mail bag.

Sibanda was in the office. 'You're going to *that* mad place?' he asked.

I began talking about luck. He seemed unimpressed; but he waved a letter in front of me that had just been taken out of the zebra-skin bag.

'Today,' he said, 'the mail bag has better luck for you.' He handed the letter to me. 'Look who's name is on the top of the envelope.'

It was the first proper letter from Estelle. A couple more cards had come from her as she moved about, but like the first one they showed stress and said very little. Not so the letter that finally arrived.

'... Lary has learnt more from those three nights in the game reserve than he's ever likely to admit. And Robert, I too have learnt – I've learnt more about Lary than I ever want to live with. And so – so we have parted. In fact, those three nights seem to have led to a parting from several old ways. Here I am on my own in this new place and I've taken a job. I've got to tell you Robert, it's through that fabulous John Duma that all this happened. The second evening you were out on patrol I had such a long and wonderful talk with him and Samantha at their home. He said I should take a job to steady up a little. Even said he knew where he could probably land me something – guess I don't look all that good as an employment risk, but I do have a secretarial diploma you know, and just a little background in biology. And so he gave me a letter of introduction to – of all places – the university here. Sounds crazy I know, but anyway his letter landed me a job as a secretary, starting tomorrow. Robert, deep inside I feel this is honestly a good thing for me to have done, only I do *so* hope it won't make it difficult for us to meet again soon, somewhere.'

I had been reading the letter while standing outside the office. I reeled back into the office waving the letter and shouting something incoherent to Sibanda, who was still dealing with the morning's mail.

'*Now* what's got in you?'

'She's free! She's thrown all that crazy stuff off – settling down to a proper job.'

'Oh! Oh! Oh!' A hand went up to his forehead. 'Try a cold shower – meantime, I'll radio an emergency call for a psychiatrist. Who are you talking about, anyway?'

'Estelle ... only ...' I read the next sentence of her letter. 'Only it's not the university that I'm going to.'

'Well, do you expect to have everything laid on for you?'

'At least she's settled, faring well, a start to faring forward. And that's thanks to the chief.'

'Then you'd better go and tell him. He's round at the lab.'

By the time I reached the lab a feeling of awe had begun to cool the excitement. I stood in the doorway holding up the letter.

'It's from Estelle. She's on her own and she's taken a job.'

Duma, sitting at a bench, looked up from a hunk of liver he was dissecting and nodded seriously.

'That's good.'

He paused for a moment, putting down the scalpel. 'A colleague of mine was looking for a good secretary, so I thought it was worth her paying a visit. That's good,' he repeated as he turned back to the dissection.

I stood motionless in the doorway. The mills that Duma kept churning had ground away any power of speech.

He lightly drummed his scalpel on the bench in front of him, looking at it thoughtfully. 'She had to work out quite a lot in herself, first. There's still more to work out, I reckon, for both of you, but there's time on your side. Something could have gone wrong; but it didn't.'

'It didn't go wrong,' I repeated almost subdued. 'And … it was done in freedom.'

He nodded. 'That's why you can be awed by the results; and perhaps also by the prospects. You might say she's at the wrong university, but things could pan out differently later. At least she has a foot in the door.'

He scooped some leaf-like specimens – they looked like liver flukes – into a preserving jar. 'Anyway, here's a little present you can take to your professor when you go; and right now I want you to supervise setting up that fence round the new exclosure at the pan. I'll be there at sunset to see if you've finished the job, so now get moving.'

He had decided to fence off a square next to his favourite promontory at the big pan.

'Whew,' I said turning to go, 'what kind of cat's cradle of a fence d'you expect me to set up today, in this state!'

I should have known better than to say that; it drew a sharp rap of thunder. 'Then snap out of it. If you can't keep yourself free to take on what's happening here and now, you might as well get the hell out of this place right away. Why limit both the present and the future by stewing yourself up about what doesn't yet exist?'

So with that bit of shock treatment I hurriedly left in a truck with the construction team to work in the 'here and now' among the fever-trees beside the pan, the scene that had captivated Professor Bayes a while ago, and which had been the background for so much turmoil when I first arrived. And when, finally, the sun began reddening in the west, I felt it time to send home the construction team and lay down the last few bundles of reeds cut to hide the fencing. Tomorrow would be time enough, I thought, to fix them against the posts. Still in my mind was Duma's touch of thunder: 'Keep yourself free to take on what's happening here and now.' And isn't sunset a time when often you want to ask, well what really *is* happening, here and now? And what is it pointing to?

Chapter Twenty Seven

The sun does not always go down red in the bush. Sometimes it keeps a searing brightness all the way to the horizon, or sometimes it throws a delicate pink across the sky. But this evening, closing the day of Estelle's letter, it was red, even flaming the reeds that lined the pan as I sat beside the water's edge, closure of the day after the professor's letter and closure of my life in the reserve.

What, then, here and now, is happening?

This is a time when the outer eye can see only a change-over from modes of living and dying by day to modes of living and dying by night, a time when both birds and bats are in the sky, the calls of the one giving way to the squeaks of the other.

And is that all that is happening?

The sun, lowering to hidden regions beneath the horizon, may prompt a lowering of awareness from outer to inner, deeper things; a change from outer wakefulness to inner dawning and awakening. Could such a changing-over, deeper sinking and awakening be with Estelle in the hubbub of a city? As my glance rested on the water of the pan, now stilled like a mirror, there came the twitch of what could be a problem. 'Oh, I feel so free here,' she had cried up to the sky, standing at the place of the fateful hyaena attack. What would it be like in a city where things and words are closed within another frame of living, potentially as bestial as anything here?

Yet in the chaos of her visit, had she touched on a state of boundlessness, of inner wakefulness and seeing which once discovered need not be lost even in the jostling of a city street? It seemed from her letter that something like that had happened. Something which grew beyond the time of leaving here and which brought nothing less than a whole new sphere of action in her ordinary world. Something that the sparkling Cheryl had grasped with the quick intuitiveness of a drama student.

And in this boundlessness I did not even move as Duma's Land Rover drew up and I could hear him getting out to check the fence.

'Not bad,' I heard him call. 'When you've failed your first year at varsity, you can set yourself up in the fencing trade.'

'Thanks. Will you act as my referee again?'

After a moment he came across to the water's edge, pulled a few ticks off his legs before sitting down to gaze across the pan in silence.

Often we had sat together in the silence. Sometimes like this, under fever-trees watching a pan, sometimes in the shade of a giant sycamore fig on the river bank, sometimes nowhere in particular out in the sandy treeveld, or at the northern dam. Watching, hearing, waiting … there would be no need for talking except perhaps when other work was pressing, Duma might say, 'Oh well, if you don't find time to stand and stare sometimes, then you'll never be a good field biologist.'

It was Duma who broke the silence. 'You told me, it was here at this pan that your professor made you jump out of a Rover and yodel like a fish-eagle.'

I nodded. 'As Wendy said, he can be inspirational. This setting helped. But now it's time for a kind of closure.'

'What,' Duma asked, 'do you think was the most important thing he gave you, here at this pan?'

We looked across the water to follow the flight of a great fruit-bat. A half-moon right above was beginning to throw its own faint light and shadow round the pan, as if light were being let through an opening high in a tremendous, inwardly shimmering dome. The Milky Way showed faintly as a soaring arch holding up the dome, its left rib supported by the Southern Cross, now resting slightly skew on the horizon. The right rib disappeared northwards not far from where the Pole Star must be, and Scorpio sprawled headlong down another rib in front of us. There behind us in the east, Aquarius was making a faint impression to complete the moon-drenched arch of the Zodiac. Was the professor a rib fixed in my inner dome? Not an easy thing to say in words. Duma also made a rib, perhaps an arch or more; so did my father – especially, it seemed, after the self-closed shack that faked a religion had collapsed.

'I suppose …' I gestured at this sky-dome, 'what Prof gave me was this: a picture of the soaring possibilities of humanity, pioneering a new creation. Which is odd, since in a way he himself is a prize example of man's limitations.'

A pillar of the current dark age, Jim would have said.

'In what way could you think he is *not* limited?' Duma asked.

Going-beyondness – it was the professor's vision of thrusting beyond that made me leap out of the Land Rover. And yet at the same time it was not necessarily a leaving-behindness, not a neglecting of the actual while seeing into the possible. You could read the one in the other, and so discover meaning. To him the individual had possibilities beyond himself; our species, too, had possibilities beyond itself – and so had that much more meaning.

'He was not limited to self,' I said. 'That seemed to be where everything else started opening out from.'

'Then,' Duma asked, 'what kind of opening was that? An opening to a dream, or to wakefulness?'

Call it a dream, creative vision; the important thing was that it could become an aim, an ideal – an ideal embodied in mankind and therefore able to be realized by humanity.

‘The opening was to an aim, to action by way of a dream,’ I said. ‘In fact the dream, the ideal, was itself a call to wake up. One hears people talk about lucid dreaming, but for most of us the need is for lucid waking.’

To wake, to become aware; in Africa, with its huge plains of oppressive heat, its milling herds exploiting, reproducing, dying, here, before the time of man, here was life; but without much awareness, without knowing itself very much, and therefore in one sense hardly existing. The time of man becomes a time of waking to a state of relative awareness, and so of relative being; the stage of personal self, of bias, fences, of alienation and self-based exploitation. We’ve *got* to wake from this, Wendy had said, if we’re not to ruin our fragile Gaia. Wake to something still only dimly seen: a higher, lucid waking – the waking that limited self might think is death – to the spontaneous fullness of awareness that could never be limited to one self; awareness cleared of bias, fences, exploitation, fog of desires and their emotion; total seeing, total being, illumination hardly to be expressed in words.

‘Perhaps Prof is not prepared to see how far the way of waking could lead him, waking into a totally new creation, into new realms of being and so of new knowing, new experience. What might open and frighten the mind, as Sibanda put it. Yet it’s a way of experience – a barefoot pilgrimage, you called it; my father saw it as the pilgrimage of our times. And as long as it remains a way of experience, can Prof or anyone else be able to stop where he likes?’

‘That depends on his programming,’ Duma muttered. ‘Seems so strong that, like Chris, some areas even of his own raw experience are fenced off.’

‘And a dark age remains clotted round the fences.’

Duma fiddled with a piece of reed, contemplatively pulling little strips of fibre off it as if he expected more from me.

I said, 'I learnt from Estelle about a source of Prof's inspiration.'

'Which was?'

'Someone known in his time as Darwin's bulldog, but for an evolutionist he finally came to a pretty radical idea: now we must progress by throwing that evolutionary past and its mechanisms away.'

'Thomas Huxley?'

'Prof must have picked up his idea. The brains we've evolved can take us on a new evolutionary path, he said, beyond brute natural selection and survival of the fittest, fitting people to survive by selecting what makes society progress.'

Duma nodded. 'We can use that brain in ways Huxley – if not too many others – understood; to switch to a new mode of evolution. But like your professor he wasn't prepared to take all that a step further, and see what lies beyond the brain.'

'The steps taken by Ngoma, Samantha, Jim Clarke – mind beyond the brain? Those steps remain inconceivable to Prof, to Chris, even though mind is the most immediate thing they experience. Crazy. Yet, as Sibanda says, you and my father still go on fighting even while following those steps – and my father admits you aren't even sure what you're fighting about!'

'Maybe you could help us out next time he's here.'

Glumly I rose to my feet. 'For me it'll be too late; next time my father comes to stay I'll be gone.'

And gone would be the end-point I had sensed on the night of the hippo kill with my father, a resolution lying hidden like some secret creature. Would the secret creature now slip away as I left here, hauntingly unseen, unheard?

Duma asked, 'Won't your father be coming here to fetch you?'

'Huh! D'you think I'll be in a fit state to talk about anything, the day I leave this place?'

'Depends,' he said as we made our way to his Land Rover parked beside the new exclosure. 'Depends if, by that time, you'll have learnt anything while you've been here.'

The parting shot he had given earlier in the day – keeping oneself free to take on the here and now, whatever the pull of an imagined future. And as we drove off to camp I still had to learn what demands the here and now can make, learn that the revelation at the time of the lion hunt was only a first step.

Chapter Twenty Eight

The learning came on a day out on patrol with Nsundu. A day of lightly passing showers, bright sparkle, air with no dust, fresh with earth-smell, rain-smell, turning the snouts of game up-wind with a quiver of nostrils, a delicately sensed perception that parched weeks were over and that the bush could be provider as well as destroyer. Nsundu and I walked with no sound. No twigs cracked beneath our feet, there was no dry rustle of grass, only a pattering shower of drops as we brushed past a rain-laden tree or bush. We could have marched all day, clothes soaked and cool.

There was no real need to walk. We were on the track that runs beside the northern fence, checking for damage, for poachers' snares. We could have done it just as well by truck, but our transport was far behind, left where others were still repairing a piece of fence. Scent of earth in our nostrils, the softened earth under our feet; better than driving was to walk in the dissolving rain, sometimes also to stand quietly and allow something deeper to soak in.

Birds on a day like this move about everywhere, catching insects, pulling shreds of grass for nesting material; a finch practically crash-landed on the fence near us with a beakful of fur, almost twice its length.

Nsundu stared at it. 'Hau! That bird has been pecking at a lion. There he goes with the lion's mane!'

I gave the bird a second look, surprised now because it seemed that the strands really were from a lion's mane.

'Strong chicks will come from that nest!' Nsundu said, chest puffed out and arms powerfully bent back like wings. 'A hut lined with lion fur!' We were speaking Zulu, and the sound of such a hut rumbled impressively as he said it.

'I wonder where that fur came from,' I murmured. 'A lion does not give away his mane freely.'

'A lion has been hurt, that's what has happened; the fur has been torn from him and now lies about the bush in tufts.'

'Then we'll have to watch out,' I said, checking that my rifle was loaded. Nsundu unslung his rifle, and we began walking more cautiously.

A little further on was a tree standing high among the scrub. I leant my rifle against it and started to climb, muttering, 'Better we look for trouble than let the trouble find us.'

I could see, when I reached the top, the fence slightly tilted about a hundred paces beyond us and the scrub flattened nearby.

'Think there's been a fight,' I shouted down. 'Perhaps a lion and a buffalo – I don't know. Can't see anything but fence and scrub pushed over.'

'How far on?'

'Bit beyond that next tall tree.'

He made a gesture that he was going to climb it, and moved off.

Perhaps if I had taken my rifle up the tree I would have stayed there to keep him covered. But I began clambering down casually, diverted by a string of caterpillars that head to tail were trailing heaven knows where along a branch.

'Hieee!' – a frightened yelp turned me round as I saw Nsundu racing for life up his tree while something threshed about in the scrub beneath.

'What's it?' I shouted, scrambling brainlessly up my tree again.

'Hau, hau!' A virile mixture of bewilderment, alarm, excitement made him speechless. The scrub tossed about for a couple more seconds beneath him, then stilled once again into its veiled secretiveness. We were left gazing there at this piece of bush, explosively charged in its stillness, the bush whose unexpectedness we so often forgot when we needed to remember it most. I watched Nsundu's legs hanging from the umbrella-shaped crown of his thorn-tree, about three metres from the ground, suspended above the void of information.

'Something hit my leg,' he called out breathlessly.

'Why not try flushing whatever it is with a shot?'

'Can't. I dropped my rifle. You try.'

'Haven't got my rifle, either.'

He gave a frustrated click with his tongue, and was silent. But Nsundu has a fine sense of the ridiculous; I was not surprised to hear him break out laughing. 'Eah! It's a good thing the chief isn't here to see us, stuck up in trees like two baboons!'

The top of his tree began to shake as he started to bark like a baboon, releasing a shower of sprung, shrivelled pods and loose sticks into the scrub below. Suddenly a patch heaved into movement again, and Nsundu roared as a warthog broke cover and raced for safety to another thicket.

'So that's him! A warthog! That's all it was! Hau, hau!'

He swung down, baboon-like, out of the tree and made a dive into the scrub for his rifle.

'Come down, baboon brother,' he shouted to me. 'What are you doing up there anyway?'

'Well what are you doing down there?' I called as I slid to the ground. 'Next you'll be treading on a wounded lion.'

'Au! For the moment I'd forgotten.'

By the time I reached his tree he had made his way to the top again, peering through its dense crown at the scrub beyond.

'I see no more than you saw,' he called down. 'The fence pushed over … and flattened scrub. There's been a fight. Me, I say that two lions have been fighting.'

'That would be bad.'

'There are too many lions here,' he said as he swung down again. 'All the young males – I knew there would be trouble soon. There's no room; where can they go once they are pushed out of a pride?'

'So do we go and shoot some?' I asked tersely.

He was now on the ground beside me.

'You have the problem,' he remarked impassively. 'Lions are supposed to be your research project.'

I paused, thinking unsuccessfully of something to say, and stepped back onto the sandy track to begin walking further along it.

After about twenty paces we came across a tuft of fur, golden-brown, tatty and sodden. It lay close to the fence, half beaten by rain into the sand banked up against the side of the track.

'There!' Nsundu said. 'Now we begin with the story.'

More tufts of fur and scuffle marks on the track did not need much interpreting. By the time we reached the piece of fence that had been tilted over, I knew Nsundu was right. This had been a lion fight. And there was enough bloodied fur about to suggest at least one of the lions had been badly mauled.

'Which lions could these have been?' Nsundu asked.

The northern lions had been doing well out of the dam I had made after the lion attack near Mkomo. There were established males and also young males, only just mature, which could either have run into trouble or successfully challenged a superior. And the fence stopped any movement outwards.

'There are – well, so many lions, it's hard to say which two could have picked a fight.'

I began to search round the rain-spattered sand for spoor that might tell what had happened. Nsundu meanwhile sat down on a heap of sand at the side of the track and watched me.

'Aren't you going to help look?' I asked after a minute or so.

'What are you looking for?'

'Spoor. To show where they've gone.'

He waved his hand towards the surrounding thickets. 'They've gone there – to die, or get better, or get eaten by hyaenas; who knows? But the spoor won't tell you. The rain has wiped it out.'

He was right, of course. I could see that.

'But – well we can't just leave them like that, half dead or something. Anyway, I'm supposed to know about all this – it's, it's supposed to be my project.'

Nsundu gave a short, slightly exasperated laugh. 'Even the hyaenas wouldn't find them in this weather. No scent, no spoor – phhh.' He blew his hand away from his lips. 'They have disappeared.'

I sat on another mound beside the track, and gazed at the stilled bush, silent and enveloping its secrets, hiding perhaps more than one could bear to think. What if I could be still too; still the senses to sense in a way that found things directly?

What does one do?

Drop a pendulum in the mind? Let it swing like Jim Clark's to where a lion lies injured?

My eyes closed in a faltering attempt at mental openness, dark now but with a prospect of lighting as –

Ka-ha, Ka-hadeda – the brazed squawks of two hadeda ibises flying low over the track made me jump as though I had been touched by a live cable.

'Hau!' Nsundu beat the ground, laughing. 'First I run up a tree to escape a warthog, and now you fly in the air because a hadeda shouts above you. Is it rain that brings on this madness?'

I picked myself up again and drooped further down the track, as if walking somehow would make the whole thing go away. I tramped on past another clump of scrub, thick and close to the track, opened here and there by warthog runs. One run seemed blocked by a – what? a log? As I turned towards it I was winded by another sparking shock as I practically trod on the torn body of a lion. Breath, words convulsed into knots as I stared almost without seeing, trying to make out if it was alive or dead. Its back was towards me and its head away so I could not see its face. And as I made a stifled shout it rolled over, lashing out with a forepaw, swinging its head round to bite. In a half second the jaws would grip into my leg. All I could do was ram the rifle butt between its teeth and try to jump clear. But the wrench on my rifle threw me off balance; I spun right across the lion's flank.

Almost without thinking I ripped out my hunting knife while trying to roll clear of a flying blow from a forepaw, but a raking hind limb caught my thigh, swinging me round to land flat on my belly, head towards the lion's chest less than an arm's length away. The rifle butt was still jammed in the back of its mouth; there were frightful choking rumbles as the lion turned from me to this new disaster. Quickly, looking at the bloodied chest I sized up where the heart must be, with a frantic thrust plunged the knife to add one more wound to the gashes there already.

The lion tried to spring up, stumbled through loss of blood, rolled back and gave me the chance of a desperate leap, hurling myself into a mass of scrub as I heard a terror-struck howl from Nsundu, now beginning to realize something of what was happening. I was almost upside down in the scratching, tearing thicket, not even sure where I was facing, but for the moment too frightened to move in case I attracted the lion.

Renewed rumbling told me where the lion was: to my right. How long does it take a lion stabbed in the heart to die? Did I get the heart, anyway? In a thundering storm of impressions these were the only thoughts as time would not move but held me suspended in as much torture as the thorny scrub.

Crack!

Nsundu's rifle perhaps was not heavy enough to deal with a lion ready to charge.

Crack!

Now what's happened?

A moment's pause, and then, 'You, Fawn, where are you? Hau! What is all this?'

I began struggling to get myself out. Blood streamed from cuts in my face by the time I had forced head and shoulders clear.

'Hau, hau! The lion, did it bite you?'

'No, I got bitten by this thornbush,' I said drily.

'Eah! This is truly a mad day. Here is a lion eating a rifle.'

As I wrenched myself out of the thicket a searing pain in my right thigh made me remember I had been clawed there. I hobbled onto the track saying, 'See, now *my* fur is lying all over the place, too. And – oh God, look what I've done … that lion.'

Painfully I lowered myself on a sand mound at the edge of the track, gazed abstractedly at the rate of bleeding, wondering how long I would take to be drained. At least there was no spurting.

'Me, I'll run back for help quickly,' said Nsundu. 'But your rifle; you'll need that – hyaenas, all beasts, they will come to the smell of blood. What about your rifle?'

We both turned to look at the lion. The butt must have got skewered onto the back, razor-like teeth, and the rifle pointed like a spindly tongue out of its mouth. Nsundu went to have a closer look, probably figuring why I had used that end of the rifle and not the other end with a bullet. I heard him gasp as suddenly he squatted down beside the body to place a hand on the knife handle.

'So!' He looked back at me. 'Is it for this that you carry a hunting knife?'

I was silent.

'This is a young lion,' he said staring wonderingly at the body. 'Truly, one of *your* lions. One that grew fat beside your dam.'

He took a firmer grip on the handle to draw the blade out of its chest.

'No, leave it there,' I said heavily. 'Only see if the rifle can still be used.'

Nsundu gave a grunt, and after a moment's struggle wrenched the butt free of the massive jaws. It was slimed over with saliva and blood, and he wiped it in the rain-drenched scrub until it was not such a mess. The wood of the butt had been cracked, but, 'Looks as if it can still fire,' he said as he handed it to me.

I checked the mechanism carefully, finally reloading and firing a shot.

'Well at least it doesn't explode,' I said, and laid it down to one side.

Nsundu looked back along the road. 'The truck will come here once they've finished that fence. But I'll run back and make them hurry.' He pointed to my thigh. 'Blood should not be wasted simply to make the track hard.'

He must have had in mind the practice of mixing ox blood into the earthen floor of a hut to give it a polished, stone-like finish.

Another shower of rain was starting to fall, and I said, 'All right, then, go well,' trying not to show I was shivering uncontrollably.

'Stay well,' he said unsurely. He turned and I watched him as he jogged down the track until, once past the battlefield, he rounded a slight bend and disappeared.

I remained sitting where I was, slowly binding a handkerchief round the thigh wound, wondering vaguely if it would help check the flow of blood, not very worried if it didn't.

'Truly, one of *your* lions. One that grew fat beside your dam.' I looked back at it again, dimly wondering what had happened to the other lion. Had it died already? Was it relatively unhurt?

Was it really any business of mine, anyway?

Perhaps only in that I had helped create the whole situation of lion overpopulation in the first place.

It was raining quite hard, and some ants were beginning to take an interest in me – a sheltered spot, with the added attraction of a meal. I levered myself painfully to my feet and limped off the track to find cover. 'Frail and floundering though we still are …' It was Professor Bayes's voice meticulously diagnosing our state of peril, our state of animal blindness, as I huddled up against a densely matted piece of scrub close to the lion. Blindness; now it was Ngoma's voice, with something he was fond of saying: 'You do not know how to look.' Yet had he done any good, finding the notebook when it had been lost? During another time of carelessness, the knife and notebook had bounced out of a Land Rover, the book filled with scribbled data on lions, now all so meaningless. Termites had not eaten the book, fire had not burnt the knife handle, yet now there was senselessness piled on senselessness; a lion cultivated by those notes, with the knife standing upright in its ribs. You do not know how to look; yet turn the eyes away, how can one look at this blood-caked lion mangled to death?

The drumming patter of rain continued. A little trickle of water ran off the track and down the warthog path. I watched it thread erratically until stopped by the lion's body, beginning to be dammed against its back. And now, does one turn the eyes away from it again, like the time I looked away from the dying cub under a thorn bush on my first patrol?

Yet, with all that had happened, is this not a story one finally has to wake from with steadied, open eyes?

Resting on the lion again, my eyes and every other cell of me knew that looking is the moment when you stop turning away. Looking is daring to enter the here and now, the moment of crocodiles, the moment of facing, the moment of seeing.

And in a chilling shock of looking (open out to the whole set-up, Estelle had called it) I let my eyes at last become stilled, let them in a way become not my eyes, nor see a separate lion, because this looking here and now is a participation, everything being assessed together in its be-ing, viewed with the impartiality of a mirror. And here in this assessing was simply to be seen the way things work out in relative freedom, according to how they started within a frame of lawfulness, of logic unconditioned and beyond things. Then here was to be seen the knife, its handle pointing skywards from its bloodied sheath, meaningful at the level of physical survival and its laws of death. If opportunism, exploitation, thoughtlessness are part of nature's perilous freedom, are fed into the structure of logic my father saw, then is it any surprise that pain, suffering, chaos get fed out?

So, being part of the death of a lion, part of the living and dying in the reserve, part of the frail blueness of Gaia, recognise what my father had seen as 'this holy place where the unrestrained workings of nature call on us to respond with care and understanding.' Care for the unfolding because it is a sharing together; not 'protect' the game against a supposed Creator, as had been my worry the day Nsundu, Makanya and I crouched round the dying cub, and the day I grappled with my father's letter, a time when the bush had opened and pitilessly frightened the mind. Nsundu had understood, had shot this little scrap of creation. Participate with the game; exalt and grieve with it, reduce suffering where one can because suffering is shared. Look, see, not in a cycle but in a spiral pilgrimage, a barefoot pilgrimage towards something bigger that Estelle had once seen in the shiver of African dusk: a continual growth of insight, and a harmonizing, a going-along with that insight towards the rise of a new creation.

Nsundu, hurtling round the bend in the truck, pulled up with a skid. 'Au.' He found me crouched beside the lion, one hand round the knife, the other on its chest.

'You, Fawn; have you turned to stone? Become a carving?'

I drew the blade out, thinking of Ngoma as I said, 'The carving burns away. What lies behind the world – the little of it revealed to me – should no longer scare.'

A world that opens but no longer frightens the mind.

Chapter Twenty Nine

Nsundu, who once had the job of breaking me in as a ranger, leant against the door of my hut to watch me pack on the day of my leaving. It was mid morning, my father was due to arrive any moment to collect me. I was frantic.

'Eah!' Nsundu gazed from the doorway round the litter-strewn hut. 'You, One-leg-and-a-half –' the name he had invented while gashes were healing in my thigh under Samantha's care – 'you, what kind of truck d'you think your father's coming in, that he can load all this stuff in it?'

Enough bottled specimens for the professor to fill a small museum.

Chris had made the same comment only a few minutes earlier. He had dropped in to say goodbye before hurtling off in a Land Rover, waving back and only just missing Sibanda's truck as it pulled up behind the office.

Glumly I said to Nsundu, 'Why don't you go across to the office and ask Sibanda if I can borrow his truck to take all this away?'

'You mean, before Chris smashes the truck? Ai!' He looked towards the office, shaking his head. 'Chris! I thought he'd leave this place long before you.'

'Perhaps he's stuck in more ways than one.'

'Hau!' Now Nsundu was looking past the office towards the camp gates. 'You'll be stuck too! Here comes your father – in the mission Land Rover; how can he take away all these things, just in that?'

And as my father drew up and looked inside the hut, he asked the same question. I had to take him across to the Dumas' house to wait while I tried to pack. Samantha was there to greet him. 'John will be here in a moment,' she said as she led him indoors.

Then the business of loading … and a goodbye to Nsundu.

As I finished loading Sibanda came across looking puzzled. A call from the southern guard post: some people had turned up in a camper asking if I was still in the reserve.

'Who are they?' I asked.

'They wouldn't say.'

'Well,' I said glumly, 'there's no point in their coming now. If they're tax collectors I'd better get away while I can.'

I was pulled together by Samantha walking briskly from the house. 'You'll never believe it,' she was saying excitedly.

'Right now I'll believe anything,' I blurted.

'You'd hardly believe this – John has just radioed in. Rock art. Prehistoric. Amazing, in the secret exclosure.'

That was the rocky area Duma had closed off after a dowser found a mineral deposit there.

'He's just discovered it.' She sounded thrilled. 'After all this time, exposed by a rock fall. Bushman painting.'

'And just as I'm about to leave,' I moaned. 'Where's the chief now?'

'In the exclosure. He wants us to come, see.'

My father standing beside her looked doubtfully at his watch.

'It won't take long,' Samantha said to him. 'It's on your way out. I'm sure you'd love to see it; I know Robert would before he leaves.'

Sibanda scratched his head. 'Those people coming to see you… tell you what, Robbie; we can post a game guard to direct them to the exclosure – it's just off the road, legal area.'

'Not much point in seeing anybody,' I muttered getting into the museum-loaded Land Rover, 'but okay.'

My father and Samantha bundled themselves onto the front seat, leaving me a corner to drive.

We set off supplied with a round of mango juice that Samantha had prepared. As she handed it out she said to my father, 'You can't say Robert's faded away while he's been with us, can you?'

'Aye …' He was trying not to spill his juice all over him in the bounding Land Rover. 'Seems to have been on something better than starvation rations.'

'Well let's hope he doesn't get all skinny at the university. You must be thrilled about what's happened.'

He laughed. 'I must admit I never expected it would turn out like this. It all goes to show what happens when you land on your two feet.'

I said, 'There were times when I didn't know even where my feet were, let alone know how to land on them. But then, skidding around on your bottom can get you to an interesting new starting-place.'

'Well …' My father looked pensively at the wilds we were passing through. 'The mills of God grind the same, I suppose, whether you go in head or tail first.'

'Charming!' Samantha seemed to be managing her juice better. She put her head questioningly to one side. 'But, heads or tails, are you so sure you know how the mills of God work?'

My father's expression became reflective; his gaze turned from the bush to me.

'I remember one evening, Robert, out here in these wilds … moonlit it was and we were returning from the hippo kill. Our conversation came round to the mills of God. And did we have any idea, then, of what we were talking about?'

'Experiences, pleasant or unpleasant; the very basis for growth, you were saying.'

'Aye, experiences. That is –' he glanced at Samantha – 'when experiences are properly understood.'

Samantha's response was I smile. 'I expect you'd say of a non-believer like John, the mills haven't done enough grinding. There are some things he hasn't "properly understood", so he comes out of the mills extra coarse.'

'Quite right,' replied my father. 'And I suppose he would say of me: all I'm really doing is unconsciously colouring my perceptions, and reading into my experience things that simply aren't there. And so I'm merely the dust that gets blown away from the mill, making a mess over everything, obscuring everything.'

Samantha's smile turned into a laugh. 'Why, anyone would think that you and John actually understood each other!'

My father had turned more serious. 'I trust we all will understand each other when the mills have finally done their work.'

Would that be a time after the secret creature had lost patience, I wondered, and slipped away unseen, unheard? At this time of leaving, what chance of resolution was there for the creature to be satisfied? I slowed down to let an ambling troop of baboons cross the road before we reached the exclosure. There are not many rocky outcrops in the reserve. They shelter plants from fire, give animals hide-outs and lookouts, privileged little estates in the sprawling bush. Only one outcrop had been chosen for an exclosure, and even this was not fenced so tightly as to keep out favoured residents, from leopards to lizards. We made our way through a narrow opening in the fence to where Duma was crouching beside some freshly exposed rock. All he did was point at some little stick-like figures on a rock wall, active figures, running with widespread legs. There were also patches of some antelope, hidden by roots of a huge wild fig. The roots led to a towering tree reaching skywards, shaken by a chattering mob of monkeys.

'Must have been a rock shelter here at some time,' Duma said. 'Roof had collapsed and hidden all this, but the fig roots have prized it away and now …'

There was nothing more to say as we all stared. I expected my father to share our feeling of excitement, but I saw a grave look clouding his expression, one of sadness. Eventually he murmured, 'The rest is silence.'

I looked back at the lively figures … and suddenly too had an overwhelming sense of sadness, of loss. Silent, gone, this primal new creation of the African wilds – the harmless people, they called themselves – the hunter-gatherers living with nature, ousted by herders and farmers, and then by the cities.

The sadness also spread to Samantha as she picked up my father's thoughts. 'It was the mills of Man that ground these people to extinction, not the mills of God.'

'And the African wilds are being ground along with them,' I added.

Duma's expression showed heaviness too. We all stared at the figures no longer as … what? anthropologists, art appreciators? Here one could sense tragedy.

My father's comment was, 'We need to halt the mills of Man from grinding like this. That is what all the great religions teach. The mills of God are another matter.'

Duma had a wayward look. 'A lot of your religion seems geared to trying to bribe your God into turning down his mills a little.'

My father took him on. 'I think at least Robert will understand that's not what I advocate. We need the mills, the challenge of universal experiences, the spiritual tsumanis, if we are to move forward.'

Samantha had been listening to this. Seated on a boulder, she was abstractly letting light play about in a diamond set in her engagement ring, a beauty, so large that we would liven conversation speculating where the chief had smuggled it from. She looked as though it was time to end the prize-fights. I sensed the secret creature poised on the rocky outcrop, paying attention. She asked me, 'What colour is this diamond, Robert?'

'Depends how you hold it, its orientation to light.'

'Well aren't these different colours like the colouring of our thinking, our orientation to light, mind-light, universal light, the source of true vision? You can't blame the diamond for separating colours; you can't blame our mentality for separating the light of vision into God-colour as your father sees it, or – how can you call it? – sacred-colour that John sees in nature. Why not accept this natural separating into mind-colours, just as you accept what a diamond does? If there weren't those different facets there'd be less colour in our thinking, and what a colourless world that would be!'

Both Duma and my father were silent. This had not occurred to them before.

She arched her hand to let light play in and out of the diamond, a symbol in her culture of highest spiritual power, cutting through confusion and leading to enlightenment. 'We need to see and understand the light that shines through us, through us all, and what angle each of us has that beams our colour. Our talk about religion then becomes talk about how to clarify our experience of light, the way that suits each of us best at each moment, sharing it with others beyond the facets of limited self. Combine the colours again into pure white light.'

And the secret creature purred.

'Reason and light,' I heard my father mutter; he must have been thinking back to his idea of God on the hippo night. Meanwhile Samantha had risen, waving a hand dismissively as she said, 'Forget about the prize-fights. Our prize should be coloured by harmonious, understanding, selfless working together if we're ever going to get beyond the fate –' she pointed to the lively figures – 'of these little people. In the true light of a new creation the call is for resolution of differences, not for fighting.'

The secret creature purred again.

As Duma nodded, my father's comment, standing beside her, was, 'So, as Samantha has shown us, we should be getting down to what that old adage tells us: Know thyself; know your facets. That means knowing something bigger than what capers about as a present personality with its fragmenting angles. From the diamond mills comes the start of a new creation.'

The size of the idea encompassed a story from a shot lion cub to a young lion stabbed, the story of an unwilling pilgrimage from a closed-off self to participation within as much of a totality as one could fathom or bear.

'Know thyself …' I repeated to my father. 'That can take a tsunami or two, I've found.'

'Indeed it does. And as the saints and sages have always told us, without a scoured-out state of wakefulness, many things cannot be known, from what is beyond self – including what we see as sacred, sublime, divine – to the very nature of self and the colours it creates. That takes real jolting to wakefulness.'

`Well , if you're talking about being jolted to wakefulness, then perhaps I can count myself a fair starter by now.'

'In that case,' Duma said as we gathered round the rock painting for a last look, 'in that case you'll be leaving here with quite a lot to tell people.'

'Perhaps,' my father added, 'you've gained the potential as a missionary of some kind after all!'

The rumble of a truck drawing up told us that Sibanda had come to view the discovery. He contemplated it silently as we told him all that had been said. When he heard about my being a missionary he started to laugh. 'A missionary, Robbie? Did you ever think you'd leave this place as a missionary? It's what you came here to get away from, isn't it? Now let's see what your professor makes of *that*.'

My father looked thoughtful. 'If touched by all you've been through while here, then what stronger obligation is there than to be a missionary on behalf of a new creation? Your professor will find some agreement with that, surely.'

Sibanda was nodding as we withdrew from the secret exclosure and gathered on the roadside to part company. 'I always say, Robbie, you get unexpected things happening when people become rangers at this place. See, now you start again on a new path – maybe even a pilgrimage.'

'Barefoot,' I muttered.

The understanding glance Duma gave me had a touch of gravity, but it was followed by a wink: 'And while you're on unexpected things, Rob, there's something ...'

He was interrupted by a camper speeding up the road and almost skidding to a halt.

'Hau!' Sibanda gazed at it. 'So there is your mystery car.'

I stood rooted to the spot. 'Dear God,' I mumbled, it's ...'

Yes, it is Estelle, accompanied by Gail.

Duma did not look surprised, there seemed to be the fulfilling of a secret plan. He went to open the car door for Estelle, saying. 'So things have worked out with Bayes.'

'What things?' I asked, taking Estelle's hand.

She looked flustered. 'Oh gee, Robert, we meant to come yesterday but the camper we hired broke down.' She clasped my other hand, looked into my eyes with wonder. 'Robert I'm going to work for your professor, and it's all thanks to ...' her look turned to Duma. She left me to give him a grateful hug.

He certainly makes the mills spin fast, I thought.

Then it was my turn for a hug, 'I had to *tell* you all about it, Robert, come to tell you right here, in this sacred place, not just phone you, email you – we planned to do that yesterday but our camper ...' She gave a frustrated sigh. 'It was all supposed to be a surprise and time together.'

'But here we are,' Gail said. 'And I'm so, so happy, Rob.' Her eyes were watery as she gave me a kiss.

'Yes,' I held Estelle tightly. 'Yes, you're wonderfully right, it *should* be here that you tell me, here at the start of a new life. The start of our own little new creation.'

There was, of course, a problem – what do we do now?

Estelle had thought of that: take all these things to the mission, and then set out by road on the long trip to our new place.

'Won't you at least have some lunch with us,' Samantha asked, 'before leaving?'

My father looked at his watch again. 'Well, why not break all preconceived plans? Today seems to be a day for doing that, for changes, and for resolving many things.'

I heard the secret creature purr again.

What changes there were, since my father and I took lunch with Duma on the day of my arrival: it filled conversation until mid afternoon. Finally we leave for the mission, Gail accompanying my father – they were getting on well together – while Estelle and I, driving together, could recover what had been lost since our drive to Nwede stream.

At the south gate we are stopped by the game guards.

'Hau! And what is the Fawn going to walk with now that he has left his lions?'

'The Fawn now has a lioness to walk with.' It is Makanya, looking intrigued.

Dakwa is there too, stooped and shaking a finger. 'Today he is not looking outwards through his eyes. He looks inwards at what passes behind them, and if his lioness does not drive, the vultures will feed well!'

They all laugh, and want to know what I will say to that.

'Dakwa, do not worry. See … an animal spirit follows me out of the reserve; a secret creature goes with me to help strive for a new creation out there.'

Dakwa's look is of inner understanding. 'That is a heavy saying.' Hands raised in parting, 'Go well, Lion-man, go well.'

THE AUTHOR

A prominent African biologist, John Poynton is an emeritus professor of biology at the University of KwaZulu-Natal, South Africa, a scientific research associate of London's Natural History Museum and a Scientific Fellow of the Zoological Society of London. He is a past president of the Society for Psychical Research, centred in London where he now lives. He has published in various fields of the biological sciences, in parapsychology and in philosophy. He studied musical composition at the University of Cape Town and has written music for the stage.

Living Your Successful Life Story
by Stephen Blewettt

ISBN 978-0-9814278-0-5

The author cleverly uses the archetypes of African animals in stories that reflect our ways of thinking, making it real to the reader. We are conditioned to think in single-dimensional patterns, but this book encourages us to think three dimensionally. It presents tools and techniques that really work and are not just once off suggestions.

Ultimately the 3-D View is a fresh and unique view on life that is really life changing and practical.

A Vision Quest to Spiritual Emergence
by Graham S. Saayman

ISBN 978-0-9802561-1-6

The book explores the origins of the human family system. The opening chapters tell the story behind the author's research on African baboons, dolphins and whales during the 1960's and 1970's, when scientists first suggested that naturalistic studies of long-lived, large-brained mammals might illuminate the roots of human consciousness.

The narrative connects the biological and spiritual poles of the collective unconscious, tracks the natural history of a marriage and shows how family relationships may awaken awareness of alternative states of reality.

Kima Global Publishers If you enjoyed this book (and naturally we hope that you did) we recommend the following titles for your further reading enjoyment. Why not also visit our website: http://www.kimaglobal.co.za You can not only see all our titles but can also safely order on line anywhere in the world.

We specialise in Books that Make a Difference to People's Lives.

We have a unique variety of Body, Mind and Spirit titles that are distributed throughout South Africa, the U.K., Europe, Australia and the U.S.A.

Among our titles you will find Non-Fiction, Healing, Esoterics, Philosophy, Parenting, Business coaching, Personal Development, Creative workbooks and Visionary Fiction.

Kima Global Publishers helps to shape and groom new writers to become successful authors.

Please join our network website at: http://kimaglobal.spruz.com/or and visit our online bookstores at: http://kimaglobalbooks.webs.com/ http://kimaglobal.co.za or if you want to get published look as up at: http://www.kimaglobal publishers.com

Lightning Source UK Ltd.
Milton Keynes UK
UKOW052000110512

192404UK00001B/1/P